"There will be no white satin, no morning suits and no orange blossoms," Eve announced.

"Also, no bridesmaids, no wedding cake, no romantic first waltz and no guest list of thousands," she continued.

"You didn't mention a ring in this catalog of traditions you don't plan to indulge in," David said.

"I just want a platinum band. A plain, platinum band. No diamond. No decoration."

He looked at her for a long moment, and then he said, sounding grim, "Purely utilitarian. Just like the marriage. I'm beginning to get the picture."

"Good," she said. "Because then we understand each other."

Leigh Michaels has always been a writer, since composing dreadful poetry when she was just four years old and dictating it to her long-suffering older sister. She started writing romance in her teens and burned six full manuscripts before submitting her work to a publisher. Now, with almost 70 novels to her credit, she also teaches romance-writing seminars at universities, writers' conferences, and on the Internet.

Leigh loves to hear from readers. You may contact her at: PO Box 935, Ottumwa, Iowa 52501, USA, or by e-mail at leighmichaels@hotmail.com

Recent titles by the same author:

THE BOSS'S DAUGHTER
BACKWARDS HONEYMOON
HIS TROPHY WIFE

BRIDE BY DESIGN

BY
LEIGH MICHAELS

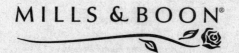
MILLS & BOON®

*First published in Great Britain 2002
Harlequin Mills & Boon Limited,
Eton House, 18-24 Paradise Road, Richmond, Surrey TW9 1SR*

© Leigh Michaels 2002

ISBN 0 263 83023 3

*Set in Times Roman 10½ on 12 pt.
02-0802-49284*

*Printed and bound in Spain
by Litografia Rosés, S.A., Barcelona*

CHAPTER ONE

HE WAS used to glitter, for it surrounded him always. He had grown accustomed to the iridescent mystery of opals, the sullen fire of rubies, the icy brilliance of diamonds, the chilly gleam of platinum and the quick warmth of gold.

But he had never seen anything like this jewelry store—a store so well known that its formal title didn't bother to specify exactly what it was. Instead, it was simply known as Birmingham on State. The proprietor's name and the street, that was all—for nothing else was needed. Everyone knew that Birmingham on State was the place to go for jewelry—if one wanted the beautiful, the unique, the costly, or the innovative.

It didn't look like the usual jewelry store, either, but more like a fashion salon. There were no display windows in front, facing onto Chicago's famous State Street. Inside, instead of rows of display cases, there were only half a dozen individual glass boxes, each perched atop a gray marble pillar at perfect viewing height and each containing only a few items. The boxes were scattered seemingly at random across an expanse of plain blue-gray plush carpet. Nearest the door, the only case he could really see held an inch-wide diamond choker draped across a velvet display board so that it looked like a waterfall of fire under the spotlight above it.

A man in a dark suit approached him, his steps hushed on the thick carpet. "May I help you, sir?"

David was still looking at the choker. There was

something unusual about the way those stones were set. Even from several feet away, he knew it as clearly as if the necklace had spoken to him. But he didn't know exactly what made it different. His fingertips itched to get hold of the necklace, to take a closer look at the workmanship, to see if he could figure out precisely how it had been done.

But he hadn't been invited to fly out here from Atlanta to inspect Henry Birmingham's merchandise and learn all the old man's tricks. At least, he didn't think that was why he was here—but the truth was, he really didn't know why he'd been summoned, out of the blue.

"David Elliot to see Mr. Birmingham," he said.

"Oh, yes. He's expecting you." The man led the way across the acre of carpet and around the artfully designed end of a wall into a tiny room which hadn't even been visible from the main entrance. It contained three small but comfortable-looking armchairs and—between the chairs—a small table with the top half draped in velvet the same color as the carpet. In one of the armchairs was Henry Birmingham. At the moment, the old man looked as if he was playing tiddledywinks with a dozen diamond rings.

David stopped in the doorway. Henry pushed the rings aside into a careless heap and stood up.

David had seen Henry Birmingham from a distance, of course, at jewelers' conventions and seminars, but he'd never before come face-to-face with the king of jewelry design. He was startled to see that the man was smaller than he'd expected—both shorter and slighter, his spine slightly stooped with age. But his hair, though it was iron-gray, was still thick and unruly, and his eyes were as brilliant as the stones he worked with.

The old man's gaze focused narrowly on David. For

nearly ten seconds he simply looked, and when at last he smiled and held out a hand, David felt as if he'd just finished running a quarter-mile high-hurdle race blindfolded, and still managed to come in the winner.

"Welcome to Birmingham on State," Henry said. "And thank you for coming all the way out here to see me. Have a chair." He sat again himself and looked contemplatively at the rings spread in front of him. "A most unusual request, this one. The lady gathered up all the rings she's acquired through the years—family pieces that have been handed down, her own wedding rings from her first couple of marriages, that sort of thing. Not a valuable one among them, really—the gold is all right, but they're of ordinary design, set with undistinguished stones. Certainly there's nothing here she'll ever wear again. But instead of leaving them at the bottom of her jewelry case to gather dust for even more years, she brought them here and asked me to make them into a piece she will enjoy." He looked up. "Any ideas?"

David smiled slightly. "I don't think you invited me to Chicago because you need my advice on how to design a piece of jewelry, Mr. Birmingham. You've been in the business fifty years longer than I have."

"Call me Henry. Everyone else does." Henry Birmingham sat back in his chair. "No, I didn't invite you because I was stumped over this project. But I would like your opinion."

David leaned forward and picked up the nearest ring. The shank was worn thin, and the brushed-gold pattern which had once surrounded the stone had been almost rubbed away through daily wear. The small diamond was, as Henry had said, ordinary in cut and color and clarity, and one of the prongs that held it was almost worn through. He put it down and picked up another. Even without getting his loupe out of his pocket so he could take a closer look, he could see that this diamond was chipped along the girdle.

A quick glance told him that the rest of the assortment was much the same—the cuts of the stones were old-fashioned, the workmanship both commonplace and well-worn. "There's not much here to work with. What does she want? A brooch? A pendant?"

"She left the matter completely up to me."

"So if she doesn't like the finished product she can blame you."

"Perhaps." Henry leaned forward, elbows on the table, hands tented under his chin. "What would you do?"

"Take the stones out. Melt each ring separately, and pour the gold into water so as it cools it will form a random-shaped nugget. Then I'd reset the stones into the nuggets and string them together with a nice heavy chain to make either a bracelet or a necklace. If she'd rather have a showier piece, then I'd make one big nugget." David tossed the ring back into the pile. "So do I pass your test?"

"Test?"

"Does that suggestion make the cost of my plane ticket worthwhile to you?"

Henry sat silent, while—too late—David thought better of the flippant question. Of all the stupid things to say... He didn't even know the man, much less have an idea of why Henry Birmingham had asked him to visit his store. It was no time to be making wisecracks.

"If I hadn't already concluded that the plane ticket was money well spent," Henry said finally, "I wouldn't have asked your opinion about the rings. Let's get out of here so we can talk. It's a little early for lunch, perhaps, but we can have a drink.'' He left the rings scattered on the velvet, picked up a gold-topped ebony cane that had been leaning against the end of the table, and led the way out of the little consultation room.

David hesitated. ''Shouldn't these be put away securely before you leave? Even if they're not collector's items, they have value.''

''One of the clerks will do it.'' Henry's smile was quick. ''That's the good thing about being the boss, and—even more—being thought to be a genius. I've got my staff convinced that I'm too busy creating to be bothered with details like picking up after myself.''

David glanced back over his shoulder as they crossed to the main entrance and saw a woman in a black dress going into the small room.

He wouldn't have been surprised if Henry had taken him to the fanciest private club in town—he was sure the man must belong to them all, since that was where his clients were to be found. So he was startled when instead of hailing a cab, Henry strode down the block to a side street and turned into a little tavern that looked as if it had been there for a hundred years.

Henry shot him a look. ''Not much atmosphere here. But the food's good, the beer's reasonably priced, and the staff doesn't hassle you to hurry, which is more than you can say for most of the fancy spots.'' He headed toward a booth in the far corner. ''What would you like, David?''

''Coffee, please.''

Henry raised an eyebrow. ''Do you have a problem with drinking a beer? Or something stronger?''

''Not at all, under the right circumstances. Today I think I'd be wise to keep a very level head.''

To his surprise, Henry laughed. ''Not a bad idea,

that.'' He waved a waitress over and asked her to bring a pot of coffee and two cups. "Then we can sit as long as we like and not be disturbed at all. So—I imagine you're wondering why I invited you to fly out here today, and why I suggested you not tell your boss where you were going."

"Both of those questions have occurred to me," David said dryly.

The waitress brought their coffee, filled the cups, and went away without a word. Henry stirred sugar into his cup. "You're a very talented young designer."

"Thank you, sir."

"In fact, you're probably one of the three most talented of your age and experience in the country right now."

"I'm honored that you noticed me."

"I probably wouldn't have, if you hadn't decided to enter your own designs in that contest last spring, instead of the stuff you've been doing for your employer." Henry leaned forward. "The fact is, David, as long as you stay in the job you're in, you're going nowhere, because the firm you work for is too staid and conservative to let you spread your wings."

He hit that one right on the nose, David thought. But he said levelly, "My employer has never been unfair to me."

Henry raised his eyebrows. "You're too loyal to say anything bad about them?"

"Yes, I am, as long as I'm drawing a paycheck. I've always believed if I wanted to bad-mouth a boss I should resign first."

"I'd heard that about you," Henry murmured. "Loyal to the core. Well, the situation with your employer is neither here nor there. You know they're hide-bound, and I know it—so there's no further need to discuss it. Let's talk about you instead. Are you content to spend the rest of your life creating infinite tiny variations on a theme that was boring to start with?''

Cruel-sounding as the statement was, David had to admit that it fitted his job description uncomfortably well. ''When you put it that way, no—of course I'm not content. And I'm open to other possibilities. However, any employer will place certain restrictions—''

Henry interrupted. ''Then why haven't you struck out on your own?''

''Started my own firm, you mean? With all due respect, sir, even you didn't do that. You didn't have much of a base to build on, I grant, but you did have your father's tiny storefront and a few customers already established.''

Henry chuckled. ''I see you've done your homework.''

''Everybody in the industry knows all about Birmingham on State. In contrast, I'd be starting from scratch—zero. Today the capital required to start up a new firm and carry it through until it developed a solid customer base would be immense, far larger than you needed fifty years ago.''

''So you have thought of it.''

''Of course I have.''

''Ambition's a good thing.'' Henry refilled his cup. ''Did you like what you saw of Birmingham on State?''

David nodded, a bit puzzled. ''If I had the money to take off on my own, your business would be the model I'd use. Why?''

''How would you like to have it?''

David's ears began to buzz. Had he possibly heard

what he thought he had? "*Have* it?" he asked cautiously. "I'm not sure what you mean."

"Have it." Henry's tone was impatient. "Run it. Own it."

David stared at him. Had the man gone mad? He hadn't heard any rumors about Henry Birmingham having lost his marbles. Of course, if it had been obvious that he'd blown his circuits, someone would have done something about it, and he wouldn't be running around loose. But if he was just quietly going kooky…

David kept his voice very calm, as if he were talking to a child. "I've already told you I can't scrape up money to start on my own. It might be a little easier to convince a bank or a venture capital firm to lend me money to buy an established business somewhere, but not Birmingham on State. The amounts we're talking about would be astronomical. I don't think I have the backing to borrow that sort of—"

"My business is not for sale," Henry said.

"But then—" David shook his head. "Then I really don't understand what you're talking about."

"I'm offering to give it to you, David. Half of it, I should say—but you'd have complete freedom where your designs are concerned. Of course, there are a few…conditions. Want to hear about them?"

Henry had been gone for a full quarter of an hour when David's head finally stopped thrumming and he could begin to think straight again.

It isn't Henry Birmingham who's gone around the bend, Elliot—it's you.

What in hell had he agreed to do? he asked himself in despair. And why?—though that was a foolish question. Dangling Birmingham on State in front of him had been like tantalizing a shark with a big chunk of raw tuna, and Henry had known it. Though it actually wasn't the business itself that David had snapped at, tempting though it was. It was the freedom Henry had offered, a freedom that he chafed for and knew that he would never find unless he could be his own boss.

The man was a mesmerist, that was the only explanation. Henry had hypnotized him into thinking that the offer he had made was feasible, when in fact…

He should get out right now, while he still could. Stand up and walk out of the little tavern. Hail the first cab he saw and get himself to O'Hare and onto the next plane back to Atlanta. Shake the dust of the Windy City off his feet and never look back.

But he didn't move.

Birmingham on State. Handed to him on a platter…with a few conditions, of course.

Conditions that *she*—Henry's granddaughter—would never agree to.

An odd mixture of disappointment and relief trickled through him. He didn't have to walk out, he thought. He could sit here and wait for half an hour, just as he'd promised Henry he would. And when she didn't show up…well, he'd have done his best—wouldn't he?—and Henry couldn't blame him.

David checked his watch. Twenty minutes had gone already. All he had to do was wait another ten, and it would be over.

But he had to admit to a pang. Birmingham on State… For a few brief, brilliant moments he had hoped. He had seen a vision of the wonders he could create—if only he had the freedom and the opportunity and the backing.

A low voice spoke beside him. "David Elliot?"

He looked up almost hopefully, expecting the waitress. Perhaps Henry's granddaughter had at least called the tavern and sent him a message to say she wasn't coming. It would be the decent thing to do, instead of leaving him dangling. It wasn't as if he was to blame for her grandfather's crazy ideas, after all.

But the woman who stood beside the booth wasn't wearing the tavern's uniform. She was dressed in a dark green suit that hugged her in all the right spots, and a string of perfectly matched pearls peeked out from inside the high collar of her jacket, right at the base of her throat. She was small-boned and petite. Her face was heart-shaped, her eyes as green as the suit and fringed with the darkest lashes he'd ever seen, and her pure-black hair was drawn back into a loose knot at the nape of her neck.

"My grandfather sent me," she said.

David felt as if someone had plunged a very sharp, very thin knife into the sensitive spot just beneath his ribs. He didn't know what he'd expected Henry Birmingham's granddaughter to be like—in fact, he'd had no expectations, for he hadn't given the matter an instant's conscious thought. He only knew that this woman wasn't anything like he would have anticipated. This woman would turn heads in a morgue.

She said, "He suggested we chat over lunch."

David scrambled to get to his feet, belatedly trying to at least look like a gentleman. "You're…Eve," he said, and felt as foolish as he must have sounded.

"Yes. Eve Birmingham." Her gaze was as direct and intent as Henry's, her eyes as bright and searching. But her face was curiously still. "May I?" Without waiting for an answer, she slid into the seat across from him.

David was glad he could sit down again himself, for

his knees had gone a little weak. He had never dreamed she would actually come...

Just because she's here doesn't mean she's agreeable, he reminded himself. *She might just be too polite to leave me stranded. Or maybe she doesn't even suspect what Henry's got in mind.*

Eve asked the waitress to bring her a pot of tea, and David used the interval to collect himself.

"I understand you and Henry have had a heart-to-heart talk," she said as she filled her cup.

"He had some interesting proposals," David said, and caught himself. *Bad choice of words, Elliot.* "I mean... Look, I don't know if he's told you what this is all about."

Eve set the teapot down. "Henry keeps very few secrets from me."

"This may be one of them."

"I've known for quite a while that he was thinking about retiring, and that he didn't want to sell the business and take the chance that it would become something less than what he's worked so hard to maintain. He told me some time ago that he was looking for a young designer, an artisan who shared his vision of what jewelry could be, to carry on for him."

"What about you?" David didn't realize until the words were out that the question had been nagging at him ever since Henry had made his crazy offer. "Don't you want the job?"

Eve shrugged. "I know good design when I see it, but I could no more produce it myself than I can fly to the moon. Those genes passed me by."

"You sound very calm about it."

"I've had years to come to terms with the idea that my talents run in other directions. So has Henry, as a matter of fact—he realized long since that I wasn't able to be quite what he needed.''

''But you must have feelings about him bringing a stranger in.''

''Of course I do. As a matter of fact, I'm very involved in the business—I manage the staff, I handle customer service, I watch the bottom line. But I have to agree with Henry. Much as it would hurt me to close down Birmingham on State, I'd rather see that happen than have it be merged into one of the companies that mass produces jewelry for the lowest common denominator.'' She looked at him across her teacup. ''If he thinks you're the right man, then I'm quite happy to endorse his choice.''

David rubbed his knuckles against his jaw. ''If you're serious about that, then he can't have told you his whole plan.'' He poured himself more coffee. He'd had too much already, he knew. His nerves were jangling. On the other hand, that would probably be happening even if he hadn't consumed any caffeine at all.

Her voice was calm. ''If you're asking whether he's confided in me that he wants me to marry his chosen successor—''

David dropped his spoon. ''You know about that, too?''

The look she gave him was almost sad. ''I did tell you that he keeps very few things from me.''

''You can say that again. You must think it's a little medieval of him.''

She looked as if she was thinking it over. ''He has his reasons,'' she said finally. ''His own marriage was arranged by his family, and it was successful—so of course the idea occurred to him when he began thinking of the future of Birmingham on State. Legal partnerships have their shortcomings, while a marriage would be safer for the business. A stranger who marries into the family isn't a stranger anymore. I couldn't toss you out on your ear if you displeased me, but you couldn't take over the firm and cut me out, either.''

''He obviously hasn't heard about this thing called divorce.''

''He sees no reason why a marriage which is arranged to achieve good and sensible goals, and entered into with both parties' full knowledge and agreement, should ever dissolve. And I must say I agree.''

''My God, you don't only look like the ice queen, you're frozen all the way through.''

The words were out before he'd stopped to think, and for an instant he thought he saw the glint of tears in Eve's eyes before she looked away. Regret surged through him. It wasn't like him to be carelessly rude.

But before he could speak, she'd faced him again, and her gaze was resolute. ''Of course, you should also understand that Henry is looking to the future of Birmingham on State. Beyond his lifetime—but also beyond yours and mine. A legal partnership can't create an heir for the business, but a marriage could.''

The woman was obviously serious. *Along with being crazy as a loon,* he thought. He set his cup down with a click. ''And you still don't think he's a little twisted?''

Eve's voice was cool. ''I think that what Henry doesn't know won't hurt him.''

''In other words,'' David said slowly, ''whatever Henry has in mind, you're planning on a marriage in name only.''

She nodded.

''Why?''

Her composure seemed to slip. "You mean why don't I want to…to—"

"No, I'm not asking why you don't want to sleep with me. I want to know why you'd settle for a marriage that isn't a marriage."

Her fingers tightened on her cup till her knuckles were white. But her voice was once more steady. "I don't think that's any of your business. Let's just say that I have my reasons for wanting the protection of a wedding ring, without emotional entanglements."

You poor deluded darling, he thought. *To think that a ring will keep men from hitting on you, the way you look…* Of course, once a man actually got close enough to realize that underneath the gorgeous, intriguing exterior lay the soul of a glacier, he probably wouldn't come back for more. But there would always be another man in line…

Then her words echoed oddly through his mind. *I have my reasons for wanting the protection of a wedding ring.*

"I think I see," he said gently. "You may as well tell me, Eve. Do you know that you're pregnant or are you just afraid you might be?"

She drew in a sharp breath and for a moment he thought she was going to throw her teacup at him. He watched with fascination as the color rose in her cheeks, as she fought for and regained self-control. So she wasn't quite as chilly as she'd seemed; the glacier appeared to have a crack or two.

"Neither," she snapped.

"That's good. I've never given much thought to the idea of raising kids, but I guess if I was stuck with a couple of rug rats I'd rather they be mine."

He could almost hear the tinkle of ice in her voice. "You certainly won't have to worry about rug rats."

"You're pretty certain I'm going to agree to this crazy plan."

"It would be very foolish of you to walk away. To be Henry Birmingham's hand-picked successor is a solid-gold opportunity."

"I wonder what he'd do if I turned him down," David mused.

Eve shrugged. "Probably work his way on through his list."

"What list?" He recalled a comment Henry had made almost carelessly. At the time David had been too flattered by the idea that the king of jewelry design had noticed him at all to pay much attention to the details. But suddenly he remembered the remark all too well. Henry hadn't just told David he was talented. He'd said something about him being one of the three best young designers in the country. So Henry had a list of three...at least.

Eve's gaze flicked over him. "Don't take it personally. You can't think you're the only gifted young man in the country. Or that Henry would gamble the future of his business on the first man who seemed to meet his specifications, without looking any further."

"How far down his list was I?"

"I don't know exactly." Her voice was calm and level.

"I see. That's one of the few things he didn't share with you."

"Quite right. If it makes you feel any better, you're the first one he's asked me to meet."

So if there had been others higher on Henry's list, they

hadn't passed all the hidden tests along the way. "That's a relief. I think."

"Anyway, now that he's made the offer, it doesn't matter where you ranked. Any designer with sense wouldn't worry about how his number happened to come up, he'd gladly give an arm for this opportunity."

"Actually," David mused, "you're wrong about that. Henry isn't asking for an arm—just a rib."

She fidgeted with her teacup, turning it 'round and 'round on the saucer. "As far as that goes," she said. Her voice was different, almost hesitant, and he was intrigued. "I don't expect there would be much contact, really. We'd have to share a house, I suppose."

"I think Henry would notice if we were living in separate suburbs, yes."

"But I don't see any reason why we couldn't be civil about it."

"Roommates," he said thoughtfully.

"If you want to put it that way. And what he's asking is nothing, really, weighed against Birmingham on State."

It all came back to the business, David knew. Eve was absolutely right. Henry Birmingham's offer presented a chance he could never have achieved on his own. It was an opportunity he could not refuse, whatever the cost—because to turn it down would be to sacrifice his dreams and throw away his talent. There would never be another opening like this.

He looked across the table at her and felt his future shift—as if he had slid into some kind of time warp—and settle into a new pattern. A pattern that included Birmingham on State. And Eve.

"Let's have lunch," he said, "and plan a wedding."

*   *   *

Not that there was much to plan as far as the wedding went, and Eve thought it best to make that clear from the beginning. "I don't intend to play silly games," she said. "There will be no white satin beaded with pearls, no train-bearers, no morning suits and spats, no orange blossoms, and no—"

"No illusion."

She looked at him sharply, studying him for the first time. He was good-looking enough, though perhaps his face was just a little too roughly cut to be considered exactly handsome. He had ordinary brown hair and anything-but-ordinary brown eyes, flecked with gold and surrounded by long, curly lashes. And the air of self-confidence he projected gave him a certain presence.

"Isn't that what they call the stuff they make veils out of? Illusion?" He sounded quite innocent, but there was more of an Atlanta drawl in his voice than Eve had detected before. "I'm sure I've heard that somewhere."

No illusions.... That was what he'd meant, of course. But since it was exactly what she'd been getting at, Eve could hardly take offense. "None. Also no bridesmaids, no wedding cake in little decorated boxes for guests to take home, no romantic first waltz, no garter to remove and throw to the bachelors in the crowd—"

"Now why doesn't that surprise me," he said.

It obviously hadn't been a question, but Eve thought she saw puzzlement as well as a tinge of relief in his eyes. The puzzlement annoyed her just a little. Did he really believe that the height of every young woman's ambition was an elaborate wedding ceremony, no matter what circumstances lay behind the marriage?

The relief he displayed, however, she had no trouble understanding. She didn't doubt that if she insisted he would have agreed to the most formal wedding ever organized—even if he'd had to grit his teeth and get half smashed to make it through the ceremony—for no price would be too high in return for what he was getting. A wedding was only one day. Birmingham on State would be forever.

But Eve was glad that she'd thought it all through ahead of time and made her decision. Their reasons for marrying were perfectly good ones, but the world would never understand them. And standing in front of an altar, making solemn religious vows and pretending starry-eyed love—or even fondness—that they didn't feel, would be sheer hypocrisy. Far better to have a low key and private civil ceremony, and let the world think what it liked.

"And, of course, no guest lists of thousands," she finished. "So if your mother is the managing type who'll be disappointed that she isn't the general in charge of an extravaganza, you can tell her from me that it isn't going to happen."

"She died when I was eighteen," David said quietly.

Eve caught her breath with a painful gulp. "I'm sorry. I let myself get carried away, and I never stopped to think…"

"You couldn't have known." He toyed with a bread stick. "You didn't mention a ring in that catalog of traditions you don't plan to indulge in." He was looking appraisingly at her left hand, which was lying cupped on the red-checked tablecloth.

She looked down at her bare fingers and summoned all her self-control to keep from moving her hand out of sight. "If you're already turning over designs in your head for some stunning engagement ring, don't bother."

He frowned. "You *don't* want a ring? Henry Birmingham's granddaughter not wear an engagement ring? Besides, it's what I do, Eve. People would expect—'' He stopped suddenly.

"Exactly. And while you were creating it you'd be thinking not of what I liked or wanted, because you don't even know that. You'd be thinking of the impression it would make on the people who saw it. Thanks, but I'd just as soon not be a walking billboard.''

"Dammit, Eve, you're making some pretty big assumptions here—such as concluding that I wouldn't even ask what you'd like to wear.''

"You want to know? Fine, I'll tell you. I want a platinum band.''

"Much better for your coloring than gold. What about a stone? A diamond, or would you rather have color?''

"Just a band. A plain platinum band. No diamond, no decoration.''

He looked at her for a long moment, and then he said, sounding grim, "Purely utilitarian. Just like the marriage. I'm beginning to get the picture.''

"Good,'' she said. "Because then we understand each other.'' And, with her hand shaking only a very little, she picked up her cup and sipped her lukewarm tea.

CHAPTER TWO

EVE arrived at the airport a full hour before David's plane was due to land.

A whole hour to kill, she thought as she settled into the area set aside for greeting incoming passengers. It was just a good thing David would never know how early she was. He might conclude that she'd been in a rush because she was anxious to see him, when the truth was that she had merely been escaping from Henry— and spending an hour in a lounge at O'Hare was a small price to pay if it meant she didn't have to deal with her grandfather for a while.

The fifth time this afternoon that Henry had put his head into her office to ask if she'd heard from David yet today, Eve had lost her temper. "He's a grown man, Henry. He can get himself onto a plane without directions from me. I've ordered a limo to meet him at O'Hare, and the driver has full instructions to take him to the hotel so he can drop off his luggage, then bring him to the store. What else do you want?"

"That just doesn't seem very friendly, somehow," Henry said. "I mean, the boy's making a big change by coming out here. Giving up a lot."

"I'm sure he feels quite comfortable about the sacrifice he's making." Eve didn't bother to keep the sarcasm out of her voice.

"We want him to feel good about the decision."

"That's why I called the limo service instead of suggesting the hotel shuttle or a cab. If you don't think that's enough, why don't you go meet him?''

''Well, I could, I suppose. But what about you? It's been a whole month since you've seen him, Eve. Greeting him here on the sales floor—in front of the staff and all—just doesn't seem right.''

''You needn't worry about a public display of affection embarrassing the staff.'' Eve shuffled papers and bent her head over her desk once more.

Henry ignored the hint. ''Why don't you take the rest of the afternoon off and go meet him? And don't worry about bringing him back here. Tomorrow will be soon enough for him to start getting acquainted with the details.''

''I'm *busy,* Henry.''

''Too busy to greet your fiancé? All right, my dear. If you can't break away, you can't.''

Eve folded her arms and looked at him suspiciously. When Henry started sounding saintly, it was generally time to duck for cover.

He sat down opposite her desk and gestured at the papers scattered across her desk. ''So tell me about this ad campaign we're going to be running.'' His eyes were bright and expectant.

Eve was stuck, and she knew it. The truth was that if she'd had to take a quiz on the new slogans which the ad agency had suggested to promote Birmingham on State, she would have flunked, despite the fact that she'd been looking at the ad mockups all afternoon.

And it was apparent Henry knew it, too. Something about the solid way he was occupying the chair said he'd planted himself for the rest of the afternoon—or as long as it took to drive her out.

''Fine,'' she said, pushing her papers away. ''I'll go

to the airport. I don't know *why* I'm going, as I'm fairly sure David will be able to recognize his own name on the sign the limo driver will be holding up. But since you insist—''

''Don't hurry back,'' Henry suggested. ''Show him around the city a little, introduce him to his new home.''

''I am not a tour guide.''

''Then take him out for dinner. Everybody's got to eat.''

After that, Eve couldn't wait to get out of the store before Henry could add to his list. And just in case he had afterthoughts, she turned off her cell phone as she went out the door.

Unfortunately, the cab she hailed just outside the store made record time on the freeway, and so here she was— sitting in a lounge at O'Hare with sixty minutes to waste. She hadn't even had the sense to bundle the ad campaign into a briefcase to bring along, so she had nothing to do but think.

And thinking too much, she had long ago discovered, could be a dangerous activity. She had tried *not* to think about David in the last month, since he'd caught his plane back to Atlanta after their fateful lunch. The idea that in less than a week she was going to commit herself for life to a total stranger was just too much to contemplate.

Well, not quite a *total* stranger, she reflected. They'd talked on the phone several times.

Though it might be more accurate to say *a few* times.

''As long as you're being truthful,'' she muttered, ''you might as well admit you've only exchanged words with him three times since you agreed to marry him.''

And those occasions had been when Henry had handed her the phone. Neither Eve nor David had initiated the contacts, and the conversations had been terse and stilted. The fact was that they didn't know each other any better now than they had when they'd struck their bargain.

Not that it mattered much how well they knew each other, she reminded herself. Even though the actual wedding was still a few days off, they were committed. The legal papers regarding Birmingham on State were drawn, waiting only to be signed. The marriage license was ready.

David wouldn't back out, that was certain. Once the business had been placed within his reach, he would have married a boa constrictor rather than let the business slip away.

And as for Eve…

She had made up her mind months ago, when Henry had first hinted at his plan. Long before she'd ever met David Elliot. Since it didn't matter to her anymore who she married, she might as well please her grandfather and preserve the business which meant so much to both of them. So she had made a conscious decision to trust Henry's judgment.

Not that it had been such an enormous leap of faith to believe in her grandfather's wisdom, because one thing was dead certain: the man Henry had selected for her couldn't possibly turn out to be a more unfortunate choice than her own had.

Travis…

Allowing herself to think about Travis Tate was like probing a sensitive spot on a tooth. The pain was no longer constant, as it had been in the beginning. But the agony of grief and loss could flare up—as it had today—at the slightest reminder, without warning and without giving her any chance to brace herself against it.

Still, it was a little easier to bear now. With time, Eve told herself, perhaps it would recede even more, until someday it might be nothing more than a low-level but ever-present heartache. And it was a little comfort— though very little—to know that she had done the right thing. As much as the decision had hurt, she couldn't have lived with herself had she done anything else.

A woman sitting nearby tossed a magazine toward the wastebasket—but missed—as she went to greet a passenger. Eve watched them walk toward the door, then picked up the discarded magazine and began to flip through the pages, hardly seeing the articles. Every few minutes a new gush of passengers came down the concourse, and she glanced up not at them but at the monitor overhead, where the flight from Atlanta was still listed as expected to arrive on time.

There was no question in her mind that she had made the right choice—the only choice—where Travis was concerned. But that didn't mean she could ever put it all behind her.

A woman couldn't stop loving someone simply because he was out of her reach. Caring wasn't like a faucet, to be turned on and off at will. It was more like an artesian spring bubbling up when and where it willed, unstopping and unstoppable.

Of course, the fact that she had given her heart so completely to Travis meant there was no chance of another love in her life. Eve had accepted that, but it wasn't something she cared to explain. Even Henry didn't know the entire story, and she wasn't about to tell every man who invited her out for dinner that she could never be interested in him because she was permanently and forever in love with someone else.

As a matter of fact, in the months since she had made

her decision about Travis, it had been even more difficult than usual for her to remain aloof from other men. The male of the species seemed to find the world-weary and obviously uninterested Eve more attractive—or perhaps just more of a challenge—than ever before.

I have my reasons, she had told David, *for wanting the protection of a wedding ring.* Once married, she would no longer have to be on guard every instant for fear that some man would think she was flirting, leading him on, indicating an interest she was far from feeling.

The possibility that she was interested in him would never occur to David, of course, because he knew better. That was why he would make such an ideal husband. The bargain they had struck certainly wasn't doing him any harm—the benefits he was getting from the marriage were immense. And since neither of them was under any illusion that their marriage would ever be anything verging on romance, there would be no need to pretend or to be on guard against a slip of the tongue or an action that might be misinterpreted.

Not even Henry was unrealistic enough to hope that they had fallen in love at first sight. Or that they'd do so any other time along the way, either. And though he'd no doubt be saddened when he realized, somewhere down the road, that the heir he hoped for wasn't going to materialize—well, even the most intimate of marriages didn't always produce offspring. Being childless didn't prove anything.

The arrangement was perfect, Eve told herself. And the case of nerves that she was suffering was nothing more than any woman felt on taking such an irrevocable action. It didn't indicate doubt.

In fact, she wished that she'd been able to convince

Henry to hold the wedding tonight and have it over with. What was the sense of waiting any longer?

Another stream of passengers strode by, but Eve was paying no attention. She was watching a man in a dark blue uniform who had just taken up his stance at the edge of the waiting area, holding a sign that said Elliot. The limo driver, right on time.

It would be pretty funny, Eve thought, if David spotted the driver but walked right past her. For a moment, she toyed with the idea of staying where she was, her magazine hiding her face, and waiting until they'd gone. She could always tell Henry that she'd missed David in all the airport traffic....

A passenger stopped abruptly beside her, momentarily blocking the man behind him and making him dodge and swear, but Eve didn't notice him at all until he spoke softly. "Eve?"

She jerked around to face him. *That voice,* she thought. *It can't be—* "Travis?"

"Eve," he said, and there was a tremor in his usually smooth voice. "My darling Eve. How did you know... from my secretary, of course. That's how you found out I'd be coming in today. I didn't know you were keeping in touch with her."

She shook her head. But she couldn't keep herself from looking at him, drinking in the sight of him. He looked more elegant than ever, she thought, his tailoring perfect and every white-blond hair in place, with a trench coat slung casually over his arm and a slim alligator-skin sample case in one hand.

"I didn't dare to hope," he said, and his voice cracked. "I've longed for you so, my darling. I've tried to do as you asked. I've tried so hard, but it simply hasn't worked. I can't stop thinking of you, dreaming of you, wanting you. And you obviously can't forget me either, or you wouldn't be here to meet me.'' He sounded triumphant. ''Let me hear you say it, Eve. Tell me you're here because you've changed your mind.''

If only I could change my mind, she thought, *but I can't—because nothing is different.* She summoned every ounce of courage and self-control she possessed. ''I'm not here to meet you, Travis.''

He seemed to falter for an instant before regaining his conviction. ''But of course you are. Why else would you be sitting here?'' He put out an arm as if to draw her against him. ''It's not exactly the hot spot of the city.''

The agony and the uncertainty and the self-questioning that had haunted Eve in the days while she was making her decision swept over her again in waves. It was all starting over again, she thought in despair. She felt herself wavering, moved by the way his voice had trembled with earnestness. Perhaps she'd been wrong after all to turn her back on what they'd shared, to deny them the chance at a life together....

No, she told herself firmly. Her decision, made with such grief and pain and logic, could not have been wrong. This momentary vacillation was the madness.

But how was she going to convince Travis of that, when she was having trouble persuading herself?

Something beyond Travis caught her eye, and she looked over his shoulder at a passenger who was coming down the concourse. A tall, broad-shouldered, ever-so-slightly rumpled passenger—but then David wasn't in the habit, as Travis was, of spending hours every day on airliners.

David, she thought, and relief surged through her.

She tossed aside the magazine she'd been holding, ducked past Travis, and ran to meet David. She saw his eyebrows go up slightly just as she flung herself against him with her face lifted to his. "Kiss me," she said in an urgent undertone.

He dropped his briefcase, his arms closed around her, and his mouth came down, hard and demanding, on hers.

This is a good man to have around in an emergency, Eve thought. *No questions, no hesitation, just prompt and effective action.*

His first kiss was long and deep and hot, the assured embrace of a lover who hadn't the slightest doubt that his caress would be welcomed and encouraged. *Very effective action, in fact.* Eve was feeling a little shaky herself, and she couldn't begin to imagine what this must look like to a casual observer.

David ended the kiss, held her a fraction of an inch away from him for a moment, and then, as if she had stirred a hunger that wouldn't allow him to let her go, pulled her even closer, wrapping her more tightly in his arms, and kissed her as if the first caress had been only a casual greeting.

By the time he finally raised his head, Eve's brain was as full of static as a badly tuned radio. She could hear bits of conversation from people in the concourse, but she was having trouble making sense of the words. "Lucky guy," one man observed in a low tone. "That's quite a welcome home, buddy." And a woman sniffed and said to her companion, "Really! Did you see where he'd put his hands? These young people—don't they realize others aren't interested in watching their bedroom acrobatics in public?"

That at least answered her question about how their display had appeared to bystanders, Eve thought philosophically.

Trying not to be obvious about it, she glanced over her shoulder, but she couldn't catch sight of Travis.

"If you're looking for the guy you were talking to," David said, "he stuck around to watch for a bit, then he just melted away. I'm assuming, of course, that was the desired effect."

He sounded as calm as if he'd just given her a peck on the cheek. And he still had hold of her arm, as if he was afraid she'd collapse if he let go.

"I'm perfectly capable of standing up on my own," Eve said.

He immediately let go of her and stooped to pick up the thick, well-worn briefcase he'd dropped when she flung herself against him. "Don't forget your magazine."

"What? Oh, it's not mine."

"Really? When I first caught sight of you, you were holding it as if you were defending it with your life. Or maybe more like it was a shield to protect you. I don't suppose you'd like to tell me what that little scene was all about."

No, Eve thought, and almost said so before she realized that it was absolutely necessary to give him some kind of explanation. "It was just…" She stopped. "He was just somebody that I thought shouldn't know about our…our…"

"Our little agreement," David said helpfully. "You know, I was already starting to wonder whether you weren't being too optimistic about how much of a public image we'll have to maintain in order to be convincing as a married couple. Merely sharing living space might satisfy Henry for the moment, but what about other people? Like…whoever it was you were impressing there."

He was obviously waiting for a name. *Let him wait,*

Eve thought. "As far as public image is concerned, we do have to talk about it. I suppose we need to go claim your bags?" She signaled the driver, who touched his cap and led the way toward baggage claim.

Eve looked doubtfully at the two suitcases David pointed out as they came down the conveyer belt. "You travel awfully light."

Without a word, the driver picked up the two bags.

"I shipped a few things." David's hand came to rest easily on the small of Eve's back, guiding her toward the exit.

She could feel shivers rushing both up and down her spine from the place where his fingertips rested, and told herself briskly not to be silly. There was no reason a mere polite touch should make her body quiver all over again as that kiss had.

"Oh, of course," she said. "I'd forgotten I gave you the address. Well, if there's anything you need in the meantime, I'm sure the hotel will have it."

"Hotel?"

"Henry made a reservation for you at the Englin." She felt color rising in her cheeks. "He thought it wouldn't be quite the thing for you to move into my place till after the wedding, and his penthouse isn't much more than an efficiency—there's no room for a guest. But the Englin is one of the city's better hotels."

"I'm sure it'll be fine."

"It's only for a few days, anyway, until the wedding." She took a deep breath. "I should warn you about the wedding, I suppose."

He helped her into the back of the limousine and settled into the leather seat beside her. "What about it?"

"Well, I thought the sensible thing would be to have it today and get it over with, and I had the arrangements almost completed when Henry got hold of the whole thing.''

David's eyebrows went up. ''Are we having white satin and orange blossom in the local cathedral after all?''

''No, thank heaven he was reasonable about all of that. But he thinks a private ceremony with just us and a judge looks like we're hiding something, so he's insisting that we have a few guests and a small reception.''

He didn't answer immediately, and she looked at him quizzically.

''That's not quite true,'' David said finally. ''It's nice of Henry to take the responsibility, and I know he thinks it's a good idea because he told me so. But he isn't the one who's insisting. I am.''

The shock of his announcement caused Eve to lose her balance as the limousine pulled away from the terminal. David slid an arm around her shoulders to steady her.

She pulled away from him, staring. ''What do you mean, *you're* insisting?''

''Don't panic. I'm not any wilder about six-foot-tall wedding cakes and organs pounding out wedding marches than you are.''

''Then why—''

''Because all this is going to be difficult enough to pull off. Let's not make it harder by appearing too ashamed of ourselves to stand up in public.''

''Oh.'' Eve felt a little flattened. ''Well, I suppose that makes sense. But we could still have had the wedding today.''

''I also think it would be a good idea for us all to have a few days to check out how we fit together before we do anything irrevocable.''

"Don't be ridiculous," Eve scoffed. "You wouldn't back out now. You'd embrace an alligator before you'd let this chance go by. And speaking of embraces—"

"Let me guess," he said without looking at her. "You want to be certain I didn't interpret that little demonstration in the airport as any kind of an invitation."

She tried to be unobtrusive about her sigh of relief. "Exactly. It's not that I really expected you'd misunderstand, but—"

"Well, it'll be easy enough to avoid any problems in the future. We can work up some regular plays, like a football team, and then you can just signal me with the numbers."

The limo driver's voice came over the intercom, sounding tinny. "Excuse me, Miss. Is the plan still to go to the Englin first?"

Eve looked out the window. She hadn't realized they were already in the Loop. "Yes, please." She glanced at David. "Henry suggested I give you a tour of the city and take you out for dinner. He seemed to think we needed a little privacy."

"I can't imagine why."

"I couldn't agree more, but I suppose—"

He interrupted. "Thank you very much, but no. I'm a little tired."

Eve frowned, puzzled. He didn't sound tired; he sounded as if he were an amateur actor reciting a brand-new set of lines. What was going on?

It wasn't late, but the autumn afternoon had already faded and in the caverns of the city, between the sky-scrapers, it was rapidly growing dark. Inside the car, it was dim enough that she had trouble reading David's expression.

He was watching her just as intently. "What's the

matter?'' he asked gently. ''Isn't that what you wanted me to say, so you can go home and tell Henry you'd done your best?'' There was no animosity in his voice.

She thought back over what she'd said. *Henry made a reservation... Henry suggested... He seemed to think we needed privacy... Get the wedding over with...*

It must have sounded to David as though she was willing to associate with him only because Henry had issued orders. *What an insufferable prig I must sound like.*

The limo had pulled up under the hotel's canopied front entrance, and the driver came around the car to open the door. The sudden light inside the car made Eve want to fling up a hand to protect her eyes—or perhaps to keep David from looking even more closely at her.

The driver walked around to the rear of the car to get the luggage. David made no move to get out. ''You're afraid,'' he said. ''That's why you wanted to rush the wedding, isn't it, Eve? Because you've given your word and now you can't back out, no matter how much you might want to—so you'd just as soon not find out what you really think of me till after it's too late for regrets.''

Eve bit her lip. ''That's awfully harsh.''

''But it's true. That's why you're so eager to get away.''

''No,'' she said slowly. ''I'm not. Spending the evening together was Henry's idea, yes. But I'd like to have dinner, David.''

Did he believe her? She wouldn't blame him if he didn't, for she was a little startled herself, not only by what she'd said but by the realization that she meant it.

He looked at her for a long moment, then slid out of the car. A moment later she felt the car rock just a little as the suitcases were lifted out of the trunk, and she heard the hearty voice of the Englin's doorman welcoming David.

Eve closed her eyes. *Now what?*

Before she could make up her mind what to do, David reappeared, leaning into the car. "The doorman's sending my luggage up to the room, and I can register later. Are we having dinner here or somewhere else?"

She was too startled to reply.

Behind him, the doorman suggested, "The Captain's Table has a lovely steak on the menu tonight, I understand."

"Sounds good to me. Eve?"

She scrambled out of the car and glanced at the uniformed driver. "That will be all, thank you." She saw David's eyebrow quirk upward and added coolly, "There's no sense in keeping the car waiting for an hour or two when I can easily take a cab home later. So you needn't worry that I'll accuse you of expecting a simple dinner together at your hotel to turn into anything more."

"I didn't say a word."

"You didn't have to," Eve muttered. "You have the most sarcastic eyebrows I've ever encountered."

It was, she realized, the first time she had ever seen him smile. The flecks of gold in his eyes seemed to turn to sparks, and a dimple appeared at one corner of his mouth. The effect on Eve was something like reaching for a coat hanger only to find it wired into the electrical system. Which was utterly silly, of course, when all the man had done was grin at her.

The maître d' greeted Eve by name and showed them to a small table in a cozy corner. Eve slid onto the upholstered bench which curved around the table and made a quick survey of the room.

"Who are you looking for?" David asked.

"Nobody in particular. Customers or acquaintances. There are usually half a dozen of them in here, but tonight I don't see any. And since we're in an inconspicuous corner maybe we'll be left alone." She picked up her menu so she didn't have to look at him. "I don't quite know what to say, David. I must have come across like—"

"An alligator," David said agreeably. "Forget it. Let's start from scratch. Hi, nice to see you again, tell me about the wedding."

"I thought you already knew all about it. Seeing that it was your idea to have one—" She stopped and bit her lip. "Sorry. I'm doing it again, aren't I?"

The wine steward approached, carrying a bottle. "Good evening, Miss Birmingham. And sir. The general manager of the hotel asked me to bring you one of our best wines, with her compliments."

"I ought to have known we couldn't sneak in here without being seen," Eve said. "But I didn't even spot her."

"She called down from her office," the wine steward said. "I believe the doorman keeps her informed about the comings and goings of her guests." He expertly popped the cork and presented it to David.

Eve held her breath, but David was obviously no stranger to the ritual. As the wine steward withdrew, she fixed her gaze on the deep red liquid in her glass. Once more she had underestimated him.

"That was thoughtful of her," David said. "Does she do this for all your dates?"

"Of course not. And it's not just thoughtful, it's also good business. The wedding's going to be here, in one of the smaller ballrooms upstairs. What shall we drink to?''

''I suppose *To us* isn't quite what you have in mind, so how about 'Here's to keeping Henry happy'?''

''Up to a point, I can agree with that.'' Eve raised her glass, but she couldn't quite meet David's eyes. Instead her gaze focused on his hand. Long, tanned fingers, the nails short and square-cut so they wouldn't get in his way as he worked with tiny gems and minuscule bits of metal. There was a small scar on one knuckle; it looked as if long ago a tool had slipped and gouged him. His hand curved around the glass, holding it gently, but she could see the strength in his fingers. The stemmed crystal glass he held wasn't particularly delicate, but she knew he could smash it in his fist as easily as he'd crush a grape.

Beside her, a woman's sultry soprano said, ''My goodness, if it isn't little Eve. And who is this, my dear? A new face, surely.''

Eve recognized the voice. Of all the people they could have run into in the Captain's Table, it would have to be Estella Morgan. She forced a smile as she turned to face a hard-faced woman in her late fifties, who stood beside the table with one hand raised as if to hold her mink stole in place—as well as to display the inch-wide band of diamonds that surrounded her wrist. ''Mrs. Morgan, I'd like to present David Elliot, who's joining Birmingham on State.''

Mrs. Morgan's interest had obviously faded. ''In sales, I suppose?'' she said dismissively.

Irritation stabbed through Eve. ''Without our sales staff,'' she said crisply, ''we'd find it hard to keep our doors open. But as a matter of fact, David is the most gifted young jewelry designer in the nation. He'll be working directly with Henry and eventually taking over.''

Mrs. Morgan's expression warmed. ''A designer?'' she purred. ''Working with Henry? I wonder if he'll turn over my new project to you.''

''Perhaps,'' David agreed. ''I hope that wouldn't disturb you. Henry would of course still be in charge.''

''Well, as long as Henry's supervising…'' The woman's gaze slid across Eve's bare left hand and raised limpidly to meet David's. ''It might actually be better to have you do the project. It's to be a family heirloom for my daughter, you understand. Not that there's anything wrong with Henry's style, but a younger man might be more in touch with what a girl in her twenties likes.''

Honestly, Eve fumed. *She couldn't be any more obvious if she hit him with a brick.*

''My first task, however,'' David said pleasantly, ''will be a wedding ring.'' He reached for Eve's hand and raised it to his lips, kissing her ring finger.

Mrs. Morgan's lip curled. ''What a good catch for you, Eve. Just how did the two of you happen to meet?''

Eve could feel a cavern opening under her toes. She wasn't ready for that kind of question—at least not when asked in that particularly insinuating tone—and her brain felt absolutely vacant.

''Through Henry, of course,'' David said. ''How else?''

''How else indeed,'' Mrs. Morgan sniffed. ''How very convenient for you both.'' She pulled her stole higher around her throat and turned toward the door.

Eve let herself sag in her chair.

David sat down again, smiling. ''*Most gifted?* Eve, honey, even Henry said I was only one of the top three.''

Eve ignored him. ''How odd that Mrs. Morgan never

said anything about wanting an heirloom for her daughter when she talked to Henry about that project.''

''What kind of project is it?''

Eve rolled her eyes. ''She's got all these worn-out old rings—''

''Oh, yes. Henry told me about that one.''

''Well, she only gathered them up in the first place so she'd have an excuse to call him twice a week for the last two months.''

He looked startled. ''You mean she's chasing after Henry?''

''Ludicrous, isn't it? She must have gotten the message that he's not interested, so she shifted her attention.''

''Lucky me,'' David murmured. ''But the old darling did us one good turn.''

Eve's jaw dropped. ''What?''

''She made it clear that we'd better start playing Twenty Questions, and fast. Do you want to start, or shall I?''

CHAPTER THREE

THE doorman had been right. The steak *was* good, though David might have enjoyed it even more if he hadn't been trying to commit to memory nearly every word Eve said. Attempting to absorb in a single evening what an ordinary couple would casually share over the course of months was a herculean task. But as the intrusive Mrs. Morgan had made plain, there were going to be lots of questions—and they'd better make a stab at having the right answers.

"How many people are coming to this wedding, anyway?" David asked as the busboy removed their plates.

Eve looked a little disconcerted, as if the question hadn't occurred to her. "It sounds silly, I suppose, but I really don't know. Henry assured me he'd keep it small, but I figured since the whole thing was his idea in the first place—or at least I thought it was—he could take care of the invitations. Why?"

"Just that Mrs. Morgan struck me as the sort who would know all the gossip. It surprised me that she apparently hadn't heard the news. But if Henry was keeping a lid on things, that explains it. Would you like dessert?"

Eve shook her head.

David noticed faint shadows under her eyes. "You're worn out."

"I've just got a bit of a headache."

"You, too?" he said lightly. "I suppose it's no won-

43

der, with everything we've tried to stuff in our brains tonight.''

Eve smiled a little. ''It makes me think of cramming for final exams in college, that's sure. No, don't remind me. You went to the University of—''

''Enough for one night,'' he said, and signaled the waiter. ''We'll start with a quiz tomorrow.'' The waiter slid a leather folder under David's hand. He opened it and glanced at the total.

Eve sat up straighter. ''Give that to me, David. I invited you.''

He took his wallet out of his breast pocket. ''No, you didn't. You said it was Henry's idea.''

''And it was, but…'' She smiled suddenly.

Watching her eyes fill with mischief gave him a jolt, and a mild case of foreboding.

''Let's sign Henry's name to the ticket,'' she said. ''It would serve him right to find this on his bill.''

''No doubt it would. But I owe Henry enough as it is.'' He handed the folder back to the waiter and stood to hold Eve's chair. ''I'll see you home.''

''Don't be silly. It's only a few blocks, and the doorman will get me a cab. I do it all the time, David.''

Not when I'm available. But he didn't argue the point, just strolled beside her across the lobby to the main entrance.

As the doorman whistled for a taxi, Eve turned to face him. ''Thank you for dinner, and everything.'' She sounded a little uncertain.

He helped her into the cab and slid in beside her.

Her eyes had gone big and dark. ''I don't know what you think you're doing, but—''

''What *I* think I'm doing isn't the point,'' David murmured. ''It's what the doorman thinks I'm doing that's important. He's the one who reports everything he sees to the general manager, remember?''

''So what?'' Eve scoffed.

''And sometimes, I suspect, he tells her what he *doesn't* see. So you can either kiss me right here while he pretends not to watch, or you can let me take you home so he can allow his imagination to roam on the subject of lovers' farewells. What you can't do is shake my hand politely and say goodnight. Not here.''

''Oh,'' Eve said blankly. ''I suppose you're right.''

''You *suppose?*''

''Okay, okay.'' She gave the cabbie her address. ''But I draw the line at being mauled in the back seat of a cab to convince the driver.''

''Funny. Nobody was talking about mauling at the airport this afternoon.'' Which, he thought, was one of the questions they had passed by tonight. Who was the too handsome dude at the airport, and why had Eve been so desperate to convince him that she was head over heels about David?

It really was only a few blocks from the hotel to where Eve lived, and at this hour of the night the drive was a fast one. David told the cabbie to wait for him and walked her to the main door.

While she dug out her key, he looked up at the building—a solid brick structure a dozen stories high and neither new nor particularly stylish.

''You're surprised I live here,'' she said. ''And don't bother to deny it, because I can see it in the tilt of your eyebrows. Why are you shocked? Because it isn't sleek and glamorous?''

''I'm not shocked, exactly,'' he said. ''But you said something about sharing a house.''

She frowned as if she was trying to remember. ''Well,

I suppose we'll want one someday. And I thought you'd like a say in where we live.''

"Considerate of you," David said wryly. "See you tomorrow at the store.''

He was silent on the ride back to the hotel, thinking of all the things they'd talked about… and all the things they hadn't. Remembering the way she had snapped at him, and the way she had smiled.

This adjustment was clearly going to take some time, because the month he'd spent back in Atlanta hadn't been nearly the shock absorber he'd expected it would be. Even while he'd been resigning his job, cleaning out his apartment, selling his car, closing down his bank accounts, and tying up the loose ends of his life, the arrangement waiting for him in Chicago hadn't seemed quite real.

Only today, when he walked down the concourse at O'Hare and saw Eve, had the reality finally hit. And then, barely an instant later, he'd been socked with a second blow when she'd thrown herself at him with that fiercely whispered, "Kiss me!"—and things had really started to get interesting.

Forget it, he ordered himself. *That's the last thing you need to be thinking about right now.*

Tomorrow—his first day at Birmingham on State— would be a much better subject for contemplation than the little episode at O'Hare….

He hadn't even realized that his hands had slipped so easily and confidently from Eve's shoulders to her waist, and then on down—not until the old cat walking by had made a nasty remark, and he'd abruptly come to his senses and discovered he was standing in the middle of O'Hare Airport with his palms firmly cupping Eve's derriere. No wonder one of the guys in the concourse had muttered something about a nice welcome—he'd probably been picturing himself in David's shoes.

Interesting, though, that Eve herself hadn't taken him apart for touching her so intimately. If she thought of a kiss in the back of a taxicab as being mauled... Had she been so preoccupied by the guy at the airport that she hadn't even noticed, or had she known perfectly well what he'd done but she simply didn't care?

Neither possibility did much for his ego. But then, ego was a luxury he couldn't afford right now.

Everything had looked so much simpler before he'd gotten off the plane. It had all seemed so sensible, so logical, so eminently practical. Now...

What was it Eve had told him tonight? *You'd embrace an alligator before you'd let this chance go by,* that was it.

He was beginning to feel that he'd waded straight into a swamp.

If the decision had been left up to her, Eve wouldn't have gone to any special bother to prepare for her wedding. She wouldn't have bought a new dress, she wouldn't have had her hair done, and she probably wouldn't even have had a fresh manicure—just her regular midweek touch-up.

But the whole show was obviously important to Henry. He'd even rented an extra suite at the hotel so she could dress there and not take a chance on rumpling her wedding clothes in a taxi.

And what did it matter, really? She'd come this far, so she might as well give in gracefully and do the thing right...up to a point, at least. Just because she didn't want an extravagant and hypocritical show didn't mean the only other option was a five-minute ceremony at the

courthouse on her coffee break. There was a middle
ground where she could still hold to her principles without hurting her grandfather.

Eve had finished dressing, but she was still standing
in front of the full-length mirror fiddling with the delicate spray of flowers which had been woven into her
hair when Henry tapped on the door. "Eve? It's almost
time."

She opened the door and stepped back, turning slowly
so he could get the full effect. "What do you think?"

He took a long look, inspecting her from head to foot.
"Frankly," he said finally, "I was a little disappointed
when you told me you'd be wearing a suit instead of a
wedding gown. But then I was thinking of the kind of
suit you usually wear to the store."

So was I, Eve thought. It would have been so sensible
to buy a nice designer suit in a classic cut and color that
she could add to her work wardrobe and wear forever.
Indeed, that was what she had gone shopping for—but
it wasn't what she had ended up buying. It was no wonder that Henry had been startled, for Eve was still a little
surprised herself that she had come home with this.

From the front her outfit might pass as an ordinary
suit—if it wasn't silvery-white and figure-hugging, and
if the neckline didn't plunge quite so far. But from behind…

Eve looked over her shoulder, checking the back of
the suit in the mirror. Though to say it even had a back
was a bit of a stretch, since the entire back of the jacket,
as well as a tiny mock-bustle, was made of lace that
precisely matched the soft fabric. Only lace, with no
lining.

"I hope the ballroom's warm." She touched the
strand of pearls at her throat, making sure it was straight.

"I think I just need my earrings and I'll be ready." Her chest felt constricted, as if her jacket had suddenly grown too tight for her to breathe.

Henry pulled a velvet-covered box out of his breast pocket. "A gift for the bride. I thought about making a pair for you, but I decided that you needed something old to wear, anyway."

And you didn't want to overshadow David, Eve thought, *or make him feel as if the two of you were in competition.*

The box was small, and though it was embossed with the monogram of Birmingham on State, the velvet which covered it was green instead of the warm peach that was now their trademark color. Which made the box just about as old as Eve herself was, give or take five years.

She pressed the hidden latch and looked down at a pair of large pearls, each set in a platinum mounting and surrounded by a circle of small triangular-cut diamonds. "They're beautiful, Henry."

"They belonged to your grandmother. I made them for her on our twenty-fifth anniversary."

"But that's supposed to be the occasion for silver, not platinum," Eve teased. "And pearls are for thirty years, while diamonds aren't until…" She saw him blink rapidly. "I'm sorry, Henry."

"I'm just glad I gave them to her when I still could. Sarah would be so proud to have you wearing them today." He hesitated. "Eve, I know you and David have had a few disagreements this week."

"A few disagreements?" Eve took out the first earring and handed the box back to him while she put it on. "I've worked on that ad campaign for months."

"And in five minutes he put his finger on the weaknesses in it. Though perhaps it was an overreaction when he suggested that we fire the agency.''

He was obviously trying to be fair-minded, and Eve didn't bother to answer.

''What do you really think of him, Eve?''

Oh, Henry, I'm just wildly in love. She could almost hear herself saying it, in a thick and sticky fake drawl. But no matter how great the temptation, she couldn't be sarcastic to her grandfather. ''He seems…dependable.''

It was faint praise, but Henry seemed to relax. ''And that's important to you, I know. After…that experience last year…''

''I won't break down if you say Travis's name, Henry.''

Henry didn't seem to want to chance it. ''I know that's all past, and I won't bring it up again—but this once I just wanted to tell you how much I admire you for making the choice you did, Eve. For having the courage to turn your back on what you wanted, because you knew it wouldn't have been honorable. And you were right, you know. Your whole life would have been poisoned by knowing that he hadn't lived up to his responsibilities. That he hadn't been dependable.''

''What happened wasn't Travis's fault, you know. He was caught up in forces beyond his control, just as I was.''

Henry shook his head, but he didn't argue the point, just handed her the second earring.

''You and Grandmother were happy,'' Eve said. ''Weren't you?''

''Yes, we were.''

''But you weren't head over heels in love.''

''No,'' Henry said slowly. ''I can't say we ever were. But you know, Eve, that head over heels doesn't last.''

"While *dependable* does."

"And it's a lot more comfortable, too," Henry said quietly.

She closed her eyes for an instant, took a deep breath, and then smiled at him. "It's time to go, Henry."

As they approached the ballroom, Eve spotted David hovering just outside the door. His suit was such a dark charcoal-gray that it was almost black, and he was holding a tight little bunch of white roses.

"Are those for me?" she asked.

He looked down at the flowers as if he'd forgotten he was holding them, and shrugged. "They must be. I haven't seen anybody else come along who looks remotely like a bride, so I guess you'll have to do."

He sounded almost absentminded, but Eve thought that was because he was taking a good look at her suit. The bemused tilt of his eyebrows sent satisfaction sparkling through her. *And he hasn't even seen it from the back,* she thought.

"I see you surrendered on the question of white satin," he said calmly. "Maybe I should have ordered orange blossom instead of roses after all."

She was vaguely disappointed that she'd read him wrong. It obviously wasn't the suit that had knocked him crosswise, only her apparent retreat from the standards she had so firmly set.

"It's not satin," Eve said, feeling a little irritated. "It's brocade. And the only reason I'm wearing white is because it's one of my best colors, all right?"

"Whatever you say, sweetheart. Henry, can we have a minute?" David guided Eve a few feet down the hall and stopped just out of earshot.

"And since the other two colors that really flatter me

are black and red, I thought it would be better to wear white than to come off looking like either a widow or a scarlet woman—''

He didn't seem to be listening, but he was looking intently down at her.

Eve's heart skipped a beat. "What's the matter?"

"Last chance," he said. "You don't have to go through with this."

Confusion swirled through her. "If what you're really saying is that *you* want out—well, listen closely, buddy, because you're not passing the buck to me. If you call the wedding off, *you* get to break the news to Henry."

"That's not what I mean. I just wanted to make sure you understood that if you're feeling trapped, you don't have to do this. I'll take the blame."

Now she was feeling curious. Was this a gentlemanly instinct or a last-second gasp for freedom? "What would you do if I backed out, David?"

For a moment she thought he wasn't going to answer. "I'm sure I'd figure something out. Call it, Eve. What do you want?"

She let him dangle for a moment. "What I've always wanted. To please my grandfather."

He handed her the little bundle of roses. "Then I'll see you inside." He vanished around a bend in the hallway.

Behind her, Henry said, "Is everything all right?"

"Just fine." Eve was still staring at the corner where David had disappeared when Henry took her arm to guide her into the ballroom.

Though the ballroom was one of the smaller ones in the hotel, it was just as grand and glittery as the most elaborate of them. In fact, Eve thought, the room was something like a wedding cake itself, with pillars everywhere, the balcony overhead resembling a layer, and the ceiling's carved plaster swirls imitating icing.

And it seemed to be remarkably full of people. Henry's definition of keeping things small didn't seem to match up very well with Eve's. As they stood in the doorway, the crowd quieted and parted, and across the room she saw David standing with the judge, waiting.

Dependable, she thought. *A good man to have around in a crisis.*

The ceremony was brief, but Eve found her mind wandering nonetheless. The judge's voice was deep and almost hypnotic. She could smell the heavy perfume of the roses, and she could still feel the warmth of David's fingers as he'd laid the flowers in her hands.

She wondered what he was feeling right now. Jubilation? Triumph? Fear of failure? Surely, even though he was undoubtedly talented, he must be concerned over the enormous challenge of filling Henry Birmingham's shoes....

The judge asked for a ring, and David reached into his breast pocket. Eve felt both apprehensive and curious. *My first task will be a wedding ring,* he'd told Estella Morgan. But he'd spent most of his first week at Birmingham on State just unpacking his tools from that battered old briefcase and setting up his work space in a corner of the second floor, not far from where Henry's jeweler's bench stood. A dozen times this week, she'd wanted to ask about the ring, but she'd managed to restrain herself. She'd know soon enough anyway whether he had paid attention to her request or ignored it to create something that pleased him instead. There was no point in pushing the matter before the wedding—asking would only have created another possibility for disagreement.

If it was too awful, she supposed she could simply refuse to wear the ring.

Still, he'd listened to her feelings about flowers. She hadn't ruled out roses, so that was what he'd brought her. On the other hand, flowers weren't a point of honor with him, while a ring was. Eve hadn't stopped to think, when she'd told him what she wanted, that informing a jewelry designer that she didn't want his expertise and vision applied to her wedding ring had been something like telling the best florist in the world that she preferred plastic blossoms because they lasted longer than real ones.

After what I said to him, Eve thought, *he probably went to a discount store and bought the plainest, thinnest, simplest platinum band they had in stock.*

If that was what he'd done, it would explain why there had been no apparent urgency to have his work space arranged and no air of secrecy about what he was doing there.

And she couldn't blame him, really. Why waste his valuable time, when she had as much as told him that she wouldn't appreciate his work?

She didn't look at the ring as he slid it onto her finger. It was neither feather-light nor oppressively heavy, and it was warm from his body. The metal band nestled at the base of her finger as if it were using his heat to mold itself into a perfect fit.

He hadn't asked her ring size, she thought idly. Henry must have told him.

And then the brief ceremony was over. "You may kiss your bride," the judge said with a smile.

Eve tilted her head, expecting a brief peck on the lips, but when David put his arms around her she almost panicked as she recalled that hot, frenetic kiss in the concourse at O'Hare. Surely he wouldn't do that again. Not in front of all these people…

His mouth came down on hers slowly and easily in a kiss that was neither casual nor uncomfortably intimate, but which in its own way was just as unsettling as the passionate embrace at the airport. It seemed to Eve to go on forever, but it could only have been a matter of moments before he had let her go once more and the two of them turned to greet the onslaught of guests as they rushed forward with congratulations.

Eve did her best to look like the glowing, happy bride they expected her to be as she received good wishes and hugs from all sides. Henry had turned away, trying to unobtrusively blot his eyes.

A group of the women who worked at Burlington on State hurried up to them. ''We're all dying to see your ring, Eve. Nobody's had even a hint of what it looks like.''

Though Eve's own apprehension and curiosity had grown into a raging storm in the few minutes since David had put her ring in place, she was almost reluctant to shift her grip on the little bundle of roses to reveal it. What she wanted to do, she realized, was to duck away from the crowd for a minute so she could look by herself. So she could be the first one to see it. Though that was foolish—if she hated the ring, what was she going to do? Refuse to let anyone else have a peek?

She turned her hand just enough to steal a glimpse. The ring was platinum—just as she had requested. It was very simple—just as she had requested. There was no diamond and no frivolous decoration—just as she had requested.

But though he had followed each of the requirements she had set down, he had violated them, too—for the ring's elegant simplicity made it one of the most eye-catching pieces of jewelry Eve had ever seen. Far from being the discreet band she had asked for, this ring positively screamed *Look at me!*

It was wider than the average wedding ring, and the edges were beveled rather than rounded. He had actually faceted the metal itself so that whichever way she turned her hand the light caught and reflected—almost as if the entire ring had been carved from a precious stone.

She held out her hand and the clerks stared. Then one of them looked at Eve in disbelief and protested, "But it's so plain."

Henry had finished wiping his eyes, and he looked over the clerk's shoulder. "I wouldn't call it plain, exactly—but like all really good design, it's subtle. It doesn't have to have fancy curlicues to be good." He took Eve's hand, turning it to watch the light play against the platinum. "This will be a classic, David. People will be flocking into the store to look at this."

I'd just as soon not be a walking billboard, Eve had told him—and she thought she'd set up the rules to prevent it. But though David had given her exactly what she'd asked for, he'd gotten what he wanted, too. He'd managed to turn her into an advertisement for his work.

"But we haven't heard the opinion that really matters," Henry said. "What do you think, Eve?"

"Oh, I think the man's a genius," she said as lightly as she could. She noted Henry watching her with a very speculative look in his eyes and added hastily, "I suppose everyone's waiting for us to go in to dinner first?"

The crowd had begun to drift toward the far side of the room, where a line of doors had been thrown open to reveal tables set up for dinner, appetizers already in place. But no one had taken their places yet.

As they started across the room, the general manager of the hotel intercepted them to give Eve a hug. "I can't stay for the reception, I'm afraid," she said, "because I have about six conventions to keep an eye on tonight. But I wanted to give you both my best wishes and tell you what a pretty wedding it was. Where are you going on your honeymoon?"

I should have seen that one coming, Eve thought. "Actually, Elizabeth, we're not. David's anxious to get settled at the store."

Elizabeth sounded shocked. "You mean you're just staying home?"

"Well...yes." Eve felt her smile beginning to falter.

David interceded. "Just going home together will be a honeymoon. And we'll take a trip later, of course. Hawaii maybe, or the Caribbean."

Or wherever they're having a jewelers' convention, Eve thought.

The manager's eyes narrowed, though she didn't say anything more. Eve noted that she was shaking her head as she walked away.

David put a hand on the small of Eve's back to guide her toward the head table. The warmth of his palm seemed to burn through the lace. *Maybe this suit wasn't such a good idea after all.*

"By the way," Eve murmured, "I must have forgotten to tell you that I'm extremely sensitive to sunlight."

He stopped and looked down at her. "You mean like allergic? How can you be allergic to sunshine?"

"Not allergic, just very sensitive. Since it's almost winter, it didn't even occur to me to mention it. And you needn't sound so shocked, anyway, because my little peculiarity doesn't prevent you from being a sun-worshiper if you choose. The problem is that since even industrial-strength sunscreen doesn't protect me from burning—''

"Then lying on a beach would be your last choice for a honeymoon."

"Bingo. Of course, I realize you weren't seriously suggesting that we're going anywhere at all, but most of my friends know how careful I am about being in the sun. So if the question comes up again, perhaps you should choose a more likely destination."

"What do you suggest I tell people? That we're going to the north shore of Greenland? Or I suppose I could just point out that since I have no intention of letting my bride put a toe outside of the bedroom for the entire honeymoon, it doesn't matter where we go."

Two can play that game. "In that case, why waste the air fare?"

David's eyes sparkled. "Or for that matter, the time. Just think what we could do with the eight or ten hours it would take to get from here to Honolulu."

Eve gave up.

The waiters had just finished serving the main course when the hotel manager reappeared and leaned over Eve's shoulder. "Did you leave anything in your suite?"

"Of course," Eve said blankly. "My makeup kit, the suit I was wearing, some jewelry... Why? Has someone broken in?"

Elizabeth looked faintly horrified. "A burglary at the Englin? Of course not. I just wondered if I needed to have anything packed and moved."

"Moved where?"

The woman hadn't paused. "And, David, you were staying in suite twelve, right? Is your luggage still there?"

David nodded.

"I'll have the bellboy pick it up. By the time you're finished with dinner, everything will be ready." She put an old-fashioned brass key on the table between them. "You'll be in the bridal suite for the weekend. My treat."

Eve opened her mouth, caught David's eye, and didn't say a word. Because, after all, what could she say? *"So sorry I have to refuse, but I didn't bring my flannel pajamas"?*

No. A brand-new bride couldn't turn down such a well-meant and generous gesture. Even if it was the last thing on earth she wanted.

CHAPTER FOUR

THE elevator leading to the bridal suite was a private one, very small and extremely elegant. Eve thought the silence inside felt as thick and heavy as the fog that occasionally blanketed Lake Michigan. "Of course, it would have to be the bridal suite," she said. "If we had any luck at all, it would already have been occupied. I mean, what are the odds of the most popular suite in this hotel not being booked for an entire weekend?"

"I suppose it would be rude to just ignore the offer, pick up our bags, and cut out," David mused.

Eve nodded. "I don't think I told you that Elizabeth is not only the manager of this hotel but she's also one of our best customers. Or perhaps I should say that it's her husband who's our customer—but of course it ends up being the same thing. Did you notice that pendant she was wearing?"

"The pear-shaped black opal that weighs at least nine carats? Yeah, I noticed."

"Nine-point-three-five," Eve said precisely. "It was a special order for their wedding anniversary. It took Henry almost a year to locate one that was acceptable."

"Because it's so hard to find an opal that size with such magnificent fire spread evenly all the way through the stone." David gave a low whistle. "You're right. Obviously this is not a customer we want to rub the wrong way."

The elevator halted and they looked out at a tiny lobby

that contained just one door. David pulled the old-fashioned brass key from his pocket and unlocked it.

Eve looked past him and was glad to see that at least the suite looked pretty normal. It wasn't as spacious as many suites she'd seen—but then the typical occupants wouldn't be trying to stay out of each other's way, so she supposed the architects had decided that making it any larger would have been a waste of space.

In fact, it was really only one large room, though half-walls and pillars here and there divided it into areas. Just inside the door was a sort of sitting room, with a long couch and a closed cabinet that probably contained a television set. Beyond it, on the other side of a low wall topped with a planter, she could see a king-size bed. Only one bed, of course, but at least it wasn't heart-shaped or draped in ruffles. Nearby, through a doorway, she could see the edge of a gleaming white bathtub.

Closer at hand, off to the side of the sitting area, was a kitchenette so miniature that it reminded her of a child's playhouse. She went to look at it more closely. "I guess the people who stay here generally don't cook much." Too late, she realized the remark had an obvious answer. *Of course not. They satisfy their appetites in other ways.* She braced herself and waited for David to say it.

Instead he said, with an unmistakable effort to be cheerful, "As a matter of fact, it's not so bad. I've lived in apartments that were smaller than this."

"But by yourself, of course." Eve felt herself turn pink as she heard the underlying question and added hastily, "I mean, I wasn't asking if you've ever lived with anybody. It's none of my business even if you've had a dozen live-in lovers, so—"

David looked thoughtful. "Probably less than a dozen.

At least, I don't *remember* there being that many, though there may have been a couple who weren't important enough to be memorable.''

''That's funny,'' Eve said. ''Maybe you should count them every night like sheep for memory practice. But don't give me the list, all right? I don't care what happened in your past.''

Though that wasn't entirely true, she admitted. How foolish it was that until this moment she hadn't even considered his past. Even that sensational kiss at the airport hadn't made her stop to think at the time—though it should have, because he certainly hadn't learned to kiss like that by reading a textbook.

A man like David... She couldn't believe that she had thought at first that he was merely good-looking. He was handsome, talented, ambitious, very masculine... Only an idiot would let herself think there hadn't been women in his past.

Maybe one special woman.

Somehow that thought was even more unsettling than the idea of a dozen lovers. There could have been a woman he had left behind because of Eve... or, to be painfully accurate, because of the opportunity Henry had offered. A woman who had been less important to him than Birmingham on State was.

But she had no evidence for that possibility, so there was no point in dwelling on it. And even if it was so, she told herself firmly, the woman no longer mattered. David and Eve had embarked on a new adventure now, and what had happened to either of them in the past simply was not important. Certainly it wasn't worth asking questions about.

Still, she couldn't quite stop herself from wondering.

*   *   *

All this was just a little more than he'd bargained for, David thought. Spending a weekend in the bridal suite was hardly his idea of fun. Add to the mix the fact that Eve was so jittery she hadn't yet sat down...

What was her problem, anyway? Was she afraid that in the close quarters of the suite he might forget that she wasn't one of his supposed dozen live-in lovers?

If she wanted to pace the floor all night, that was her privilege. As for David, he'd just as soon be comfortable.

He walked across the suite, opened the door of the closet, and felt like hitting himself in the head for being a dunce. No wonder she was uneasy—a good portion of the reason for her distress was staring him in the face. On one side of the closet hung a neat row of his suits, shirts, and casual clothes. On the other side were just two hangers, one holding a long, full khaki skirt and the other a coordinating striped blouse. That and the suit she was wearing were the only clothes she had with her.

"I imagine you'd be more comfortable if you weren't wearing that suit," he said.

Her footsteps had been hushed on the deep carpet, but now the sound stopped altogether. "That depends." Her voice was wary.

"Dammit, Eve, I was offering you a pair of pajamas, not making a pass." He opened drawers till he found where the maid had stashed the rest of his clothes and thrust a set of blue plaid pajamas at her. "Here—use them or not, it doesn't matter to me. I'm going to change and then you can lock yourself in the bathroom for the rest of the night if you like."

She looked at the pajamas and then up at him. "These look brand new, David."

Doesn't the woman have a clue? "Well, yes," he said

wryly. "That's because they *are* new. I thought since we'll be sharing a roof from now on, you might be more comfortable if I didn't rely on my regular nighttime garb."

She turned very pink. No wonder she tried to avoid overexposure to the sun, he thought. With that fair skin, she'd broil like a lobster.

"Thanks," she said quietly.

He put on sweats and a T-shirt, and while he was hanging up his suit Eve disappeared into the bathroom. He heard the lock click and shook his head wryly. She'd taken him at his word, but she might as well not have bothered. What sort of guy did she think he was, anyway? Besides, if he'd wanted to go into that bathroom— which of course he didn't—that flimsy lock wouldn't stop him.

He opened the cabinet that held the television and dropped onto the couch with the remote control in his hand. There must be something on that would be worth watching, he thought, unless nobody had ever bothered to hook up the set. The average honeymooning couple would probably never have noticed.

The choices were pretty thin and he was debating the merits of an ancient movie versus a tennis match between two unseeded Albanians when there was a timid tap at the door. Frowning, he tossed the remote aside and went to answer it.

A bellboy thrust a big flat box at him. "Delivery for Mrs. Elliot."

Mrs. Elliot. It was going to take a little time for him to get used to that.

David reached for his wallet and realized he'd left it on top of the bureau. But before he could go get it, the bellboy had already vanished into the waiting elevator.

David couldn't blame him for ducking out. The staff was probably wary of knocking on the door of the bridal suite at any time of the day or night because they never knew what sort of answer they'd get. Still, the guy hadn't even waited for a tip, and surely that was odd.

Feeling skeptical, David inspected the package. It was neatly wrapped in heavy, glossy beige paper that looked more like a rich fabric. It weighed almost nothing, it wasn't ticking, and it didn't smell like gunpowder. Short of running it through an X-ray, he didn't see what else he could do to make certain it wasn't explosive.

He put the box under his arm, strolled across the room to the bathroom door, and knocked. "Your package has arrived."

Only silence answered. He was starting to wonder if Eve had gone to sleep in the bathtub when she said, through the door, "I wasn't expecting a package. You know that."

"Well, you've got one. I'm only the delivery boy." He shifted the box until he was holding it like a butler's tray, and spotted a discreet gold label on one corner. "It's from...let me look closer. It says Milady Lingerie."

"Oh, my—that just tears it." Eve's voice was almost a wail. Seconds later she pulled open the door.

She'd definitely been in the tub, for he could see the bubbles still frothing in the water behind her, and a clump of suds was clinging to her earlobe. Her hair was still pinned atop her head with the flowery clip, but the ends had started to come loose, and they had grown damp and curly in the warm, humid air. She was wrapped in an oversize white terry robe, one of a pair that he'd noticed hanging on the back of the door. She'd obviously put it on in a hurry because it wasn't quite straight, and the neckline offered a tempting glimpse of the shadowed, creamy-white valley between her breasts.

He tried not to look as he handed her the box. She stared at it, and then at him, with distrust. "I don't see how she'd have had time," she murmured.

"Who? The hotel manager?" He leaned against the doorjamb and folded his arms to wait, too curious even to consider walking away.

Eve tore the paper loose and lifted the lid off the box. Whatever was inside was swathed in beige tissue that matched the wrapping, and atop the paper was an envelope. She opened it first. "Oh," she said with a note of relief. "It's from all the women who work at Birmingham on State. They must have brought the package to the wedding but then decided to send it up here when they heard about the bridal suite. Thoughtful of them, but—" She put the card back on top of the tissue paper with an air of finality.

Feeling perverse, David suggested, "You'd better at least check out what they bought for you."

"I don't have to look because I already know what's inside—at least in principle. And you've obviously never been inside a Milady Lingerie store or you wouldn't have to ask."

"Don't be so certain I haven't. It's sexy lingerie, of course—but I think they'll expect that both of us will know what this particular item looks like." He added thoughtfully, "Though I suppose we could tell them that we didn't bother with it. I mean, on a honeymoon, who needs sexy—"

Eve cut him off. "Since you insist..." She folded back the tissue paper and lifted out a mass of white lace. With a quick shake she held it out in front of her.

David found himself face-to-face with a negligee so

sheer that it looked like a spider web and so transparent that he could see her perfectly well even though he was looking through both the front and back of the thing. If she'd been wearing it instead of holding it out at arm's length…

He wouldn't have needed an imagination, that was sure. So much for the package not being explosive. It might as well have been crammed with dynamite.

He didn't realize he'd given a low whistle until he saw Eve's eyes darken. ''Oh, for heaven's sake,'' she said crossly. ''It's only a robe.''

Only a robe? he thought, half-dazed. *She's nuts.*

''Beautiful, but totally impractical,'' Eve said. Her voice echoed in his ears as if she was a long way away. ''A woman would freeze, wearing this kind of thing.''

David thought that was extremely unlikely, since any man worth his salt would be delighted to keep her warm.

''An incredibly silly thing to buy,'' she went on. ''And a waste of expensive lace. Don't you agree?'' She held the negligee up a little higher. ''David?'' She sounded suspicious.

''Of course,'' he managed. ''Definitely a waste.'' *But not of lace—because there's not enough of it there to matter.*

She crumpled the negligee back in the box. ''Well— thanks for bringing it to me.''

David realized he was still blocking the door, and backed hastily away. He didn't realize until he was back on the couch that the humid heat of the bathroom had been taking its toll on him, just as it had curled Eve's hair. He seemed to be having a little trouble breathing properly.

She was right about one thing, he thought. The women of Birmingham on State had definitely thrown away their money. Giving the sexiest negligee in seven states to a woman who enjoyed impersonating a glacier…

Though when she'd been in his arms at the airport a few days ago, she hadn't exactly acted like a glacier. And tonight, right after the judge had pronounced them married…

He'd had every intention of brushing her lips lightly in a formal, official kiss. But then he'd touched her, and before he could stop himself he'd drawn her close. It was his curiosity which was at fault, he thought. He'd just had to see whether he'd been right about the glacier having a few deep fissures here and there—and heaven knew if he'd tried to kiss her like that in a less public setting, she'd have slapped his face.

But he hadn't gotten his answer. She'd stayed almost passive in his embrace, and yet there had been a flicker of response that intrigued him. Had it been real, or had she simply been performing once more for an audience?

She came out of the bathroom, wrapped more carefully now in the oversize white terry robe. He hadn't noticed before how long it was on her. *But then you were observing other things, weren't you, Elliot?*

The robe stopped only a few inches above her ankles, and he could see that she'd rolled up the bottom of his pajama pants into floppy cuffs. She must have had to pull the drawstring waist as tight as it would go, too.

She stopped halfway across the room to try—without success—to contain a yawn. ''Even my lips are tired,'' she muttered. ''From smiling so much, I mean.''

David knew exactly what she meant and that she hadn't intended the comment as any kind of an enticement. Still, he found himself staring at her mouth. She didn't need cosmetic tricks to make it beautiful, he thought. And he'd bet he could kiss the tiredness away....

She yawned again. "I suppose it would be only sporting to flip a coin to see who gets the bed."

"Or cut the cards. It's too bad we don't have a deck."

"Call room service. No, on second thought—don't. The whole hotel would buzz with the story about the newlyweds who needed a deck of cards for entertainment."

"I could tell them we're playing strip poker," David offered.

"Anyway, I have a better idea. You take the bed, because you're too tall to stretch out on the couch. I need a favor, David, if you don't mind." She touched the spray of flowers in her hair. "I can't get this silly thing out. My stylist must have used a gallon of hair spray and when I try, I just tangle it worse." She sat down on the edge of the couch next to him, her back very straight.

He was used to much more delicate work, so there was no reason unwrapping a silly hair ornament should make him feel clumsy. Unless it was the delicate scent of lilac that still clung to her from the bubble bath. Or the seductive curve of her neck, tempting him to lean just a little closer...

Not a good idea, he told himself. *Think about something else.*

"Now I wish you hadn't been so hard-headed about the little boxes of wedding cake for everybody to take home," he said. "I could eat about four of them right now." The spray of flowers dropped into his hand, and her hair fell in glossy waves around her face as she turned to smile at him.

She was most dangerous by far, he thought, when she was smiling.

Eve hadn't intended to allow herself to fall into a deep sleep. That was one of the reasons she'd offered to spend the night on the couch, though it was quite true that she'd be marginally more comfortable there than David would have been. But she'd apparently been even more tired than she'd realized. She remembered watching a few minutes of what must have been the oldest movie still in circulation. And she had a vague recollection of David lifting her feet onto the couch, putting a pillow under her head, and tucking a blanket around her. But that was all she knew, until she woke with a stiff neck to see morning light streaming in through the wide windows which overlooked Lake Michigan.

The next thing she saw was David. He was asleep, slumped in the corner of the couch with his head propped against the padded back and her feet in his lap, and he'd obviously been there all night. Had the movie put him to sleep as well? But the television set had been turned off. Surely, she thought, he hadn't been idiot enough to *choose* to sleep sitting up on the couch!

She tried to get up without disturbing him, but as soon as she moved, David opened his eyes. So she stayed on the couch, pulling her feet up under her and wrapping her arms around her knees. ''Why didn't you go to bed?'' she asked. ''And please don't tell me it's because you were being a gentleman.''

''All right, since you don't want to hear it.'' His voice was low and a little gravelly.

''Because it was my choice to take the couch, and it was just plain silly for you to be uncomfortable, too.''

''I'd have been even more uncomfortable if I'd left

you here while I wallowed in king-size luxury.'' He stood up, stretching, and she watched muscles ripple under the thin T-shirt. ''What's for breakfast, wife?''

''Why are you asking me?''

''Because you said you didn't want me acting like a gentleman, so I'll try being a reactionary chauvinist and see if you like that any better.''

''That's not what I...'' Eve gave up. ''The room service menu must be around here somewhere. What do you want to do today?'' She bit her lip. ''I mean, we have a whole day to kill—''

She wasn't making things any better. But David didn't seem to notice the suggestiveness in the question, which made her feel even sillier.

''Since it's out of the question to lie on the beach, I'll leave the choice to you.'' David paged through the menu. ''What do you want to eat?''

''Coffee, please.''

''That's all?''

''I don't eat breakfast.''

''No wonder you're snappish in the morning.''

''If you think this is snappish, don't get in my way when I'm running late for work.''

''I'll keep that in mind.'' He sat on the arm of the couch and pulled the telephone closer.

Eve tightened the belt of her terry robe, which had worked loose overnight, and carried her pillow over to the bed. David had folded the bedspread back neatly, but she pulled it halfway off and gave the top sheet and blanket a hard tug so the corner trailed on the floor.

''What are you doing?'' David asked as he put the phone down.

''Creating an illusion for the housekeepers by making

it appear that we used the bed.'' She stepped back to inspect her handiwork. ''What do you think?''

He came to stand beside her. ''Not very convincing.''

''That's what I was afraid of. But what else can I—''

Before she could finish her sentence, David pulled the blankets back, then picked her up and tossed her into the middle of the bed.

Eve squeaked, but before she could slide off the other edge David was beside her. Instead of making any move to touch her, however, he rolled a couple of times, punched at the pillow, and tugged the bottom sheet loose so it was crumpled under him. Then he propped himself on one elbow and looked down at her, his face no more than six inches above hers. ''What's the matter, sweetheart? Did you think I had something else in mind?''

Eve wanted to growl.

With the grace of a gymnast, David sprang back to his feet. ''Anytime you want help rumpling a bed, just yell.''

Eve gathered the little dignity she still possessed, stood up, and took her clothes from the closet.

What is wrong with you? she fumed as she shut herself in the bathroom to dress. To practically go into cardiac arrest over something as crazy as that....

When she came out of the bathroom, David was sitting on the couch with the morning newspaper. Beside him was a cart loaded with scrambled eggs, toast, hash brown potatoes, bacon, sausage, waffles, fruit, coffee, and a bottle of champagne.

Eve stopped short at the sight. ''Did you order all that?''

''Not exactly.'' David folded the newspaper and laid it aside. ''This is the standard-issue bridal suite breakfast. At least that's what the waiter who delivered it told me.''

''You're sure he didn't mix it up with a cart that was intended for a roomful of marathon runners?''

''Absolutely. Serious runners wouldn't drink the champagne.''

Eve poured herself a cup of coffee and sat down. ''What kind of a barbarian can eat that way in the morning?''

''You don't really want me to answer that. Besides, it's hardly morning anymore, so let's call it an early lunch instead.'' He took the champagne bottle out of the ice-filled cooler and wiped it off with a napkin, then popped the cork with a pleasant little hiss and handed Eve a glass. ''Unless you have other activities in mind.''

There wasn't even a hint of sensuality in his voice, so it was beyond Eve to understand why she had to use all her self-control to keep from looking past him to the bed. ''I thought I'd take you on the tour of the city that Henry wanted you to have.'' *Anything to get out of the bridal suite.* ''We can walk through the Loop, then take a cab out to Lincoln Park to give you a taste of the Historical Society. We can even go to the top of the Sears Tower if you're feeling like a tourist.''

''By all means.'' He handed her a plate. ''An ambitious program like that means you'll need fuel. Want a section of the newspaper to go with it?''

Eve had to admit that the scent of Belgian waffles was tempting. Besides, even the fairly elaborate program she'd outlined wouldn't take up the entire day. With all the hours they had to kill before the weekend was over and they could go back to work, she could think of worse occupations than companionably reading the newspaper.

At least it meant they didn't have to make conversation for a while.

Every single place they went, it seemed to David, they encountered someone Eve knew. At the Art Institute, they ran into an elderly woman drenched in diamonds; David didn't remember seeing the woman at the wedding but he definitely recognized the diamonds.

Between trying on dresses at the Tyler-Royale department store on the Magnificent Mile, Eve introduced him to the department head and three women who were looking through the racks.

She paid for her dress and arranged for it to be delivered to the hotel. "At least I'll have something to wear tomorrow," she said. "Now what?"

"Quite the social butterfly, aren't you?"

She looked at him in astonishment. "Of course not. I don't have time."

"You mean all these people are customers?"

"Most of them. Some would just like to be, but they come in every now and then to look. Birmingham on State is considered to be one of the tourist attractions of the Loop, along with the Marshall Field clock and the Picasso sculpture down by City Hall. Why? Are you recalculating the scope of Henry's business?" Her voice was dry, and she didn't wait for an answer. "I think we'll go to the natural history museum next. They've got a terrific collection of gems."

"Just what I want to do on my day off," David muttered. But she took him anyway.

In the jewel room, they met a young couple whom David remembered seeing in the store the previous week. They'd been looking at engagement rings but hadn't selected one.

He watched the young woman steal a glance at Eve's left hand, and the look of disappointment which washed across her face made his gut tighten. "But I thought you'd have a wonderful ring," she mourned. "I mean… Oh, gee, I didn't intend that to sound—"

"I think this *is* a wonderful ring," Eve said gently. "And really, you know, if I wore an emerald the size of a traffic light to work, everything else in the store would look shabby by comparison."

As they left the museum, David said, "That was nice of you—even if it wasn't true."

Eve shrugged. "Well, that may not have been the main reason I turned down a fancy ring, but I wasn't exactly lying. Any ring I wore would probably make what they can afford look awfully cheap."

"I meant the other part."

She looked puzzled. "You mean about it being a wonderful ring?" She held out her hand, and the beveled platinum caught the sunlight. She walked on a few steps and said, very quietly, "It is wonderful, David."

"You didn't seem to think so last night."

"Last night I thought you'd done it intentionally— created something attention-grabbing, I mean—just to show me that I couldn't dictate to you."

"And now?" He'd intended it to be a casual question, but there was a catch in his breath.

She hesitated. "Now I think you probably couldn't make anything that wasn't."

Feeling oddly comforted, he found himself reaching for her hand.

She raised it to wave down a taxi. "Henry obviously made his choice very carefully," she said.

David pulled back.

She seemed oblivious. "Do you still want to see the view from the Sears Tower?"

They watched the sun set from atop the skyscraper and finally—with no other excuse to stay out—went back to the hotel.

The doorman was obviously relieved to see them. "No one could figure out where you'd gone," he said. "The room service people have been looking for you."

"Why?" Eve asked lightly. "Is there a fine for not finishing breakfast?"

"No, they wanted to know when you'd like dinner served."

"I thought we'd just go to the Captain's Table tonight."

"Oh, no, Miss…ma'am. Your grandfather made arrangements for Chateaubriand, I believe. I'll call room service and tell them you've returned."

In the elevator Eve said, "It feels like we've been caught violating curfew. You know, I actually considered ducking out tonight after all, but I thought the problem would be getting past all the staff if we were carrying suitcases. It didn't occur to me that Henry would take a hand. I suppose the next thing he'll do is show up with a limo in the morning, with the excuse that we shouldn't have to deal with luggage." She yawned. "I'm dead tired. That couch is not the most comfortable in the world."

"It's your turn to have the bed anyway."

She fixed him with a look. "Stay on your half, and we'll share."

David knew he must have looked as startled as he felt.

"I'm only trying to be sensible," Eve said. "We have

to go to work tomorrow, and we can't show up looking haggard.''

David couldn't resist. ''Why not? The staff would be disappointed if we appeared too well-rested.''

She stuck her tongue out at him, and he laughed.

CHAPTER FIVE

DAVID took a long, steamy shower, and by the time he was finished, Eve was already in bed. She had propped herself up against a stack of pillows, drawing up her knees to form a makeshift desk for her notepad. And, he noted, though she'd taken off the bulky white terry robe, she'd turned up the collar and lapels of his pajama jacket to cover as much of herself as possible. Somehow the shadows cast by the bedside lamp, the only light burning in the suite, made the view even more intriguing.

She looked up from her notes. "Why are you just standing there staring at me?"

David decided it would be prudent not to tell her that her attempt at modesty only drew attention to what, on her, was still a very plunging neckline. "You apparently have a preference for that side of the bed."

"Not particularly. Why? Do you want it? If you've gotten accustomed to it through a dozen live-in lovers—"

"I thought I told you it wasn't quite that many."

"*Nearly* a dozen lovers," Eve corrected tartly, "then I'll... No, on second thought, I won't move to the other side. It'll do you good to be thrown out of your routine, and you'll be less likely to forget that I'm not number thirteen. Or whatever."

Not a chance, David thought. "You seem to have taken care of that problem as well." He pointed at the tightly rolled blanket that she'd placed precisely in the center of the bed. "I wonder if it's me you don't trust, or yourself.'' He didn't wait for an answer but tossed back the blankets on his side and climbed in. ''What are you doing, anyway? Writing letters?''

''Making my things-to-do list for tomorrow.''

''Give it a rest, Eve.'' He yawned and punched at his pillow, turned his back to her and closed his eyes. After spending last night on the couch, he'd probably fall asleep instantly and not even move all night. So much for her blanket barricade; she might as well not have wasted the effort.

But oblivion eluded him. The suite was so quiet that he could hear the light rhythm of her breathing, the quiet rustle of his pajamas as she moved, and even the scratch of her pen against the paper. He lay absolutely still, listening.

Finally she finished her list, put the notepad aside, and reached over to turn out the bedside lamp. Though he wasn't even looking at her, he could picture the pajama sleeve falling back from a delicate wrist as she stretched out her hand to the switch. He could imagine the jacket's neckline gaping... She lay down very slowly and carefully. Obviously she was trying not to disturb him.

That was a laugh, he thought. She was disturbing him just by being there. He could still hear every quiet breath, and every infinitesimal shift she made seemed to vibrate the mattress.

David lay still and considered relocating. Maybe the couch hadn't been so bad after all. At least from across the room he wouldn't be able to feel every movement she made.

But dammit, a man had his pride to consider. To move would be to admit defeat. If he shifted himself to the couch, he might as well run up a white flag and be done with it.

And he wouldn't do that. He was absolutely not going to acknowledge that this was getting to him. That *she* was getting to him.

What was the matter with him, anyway? He had agreed to the conditions she'd put on their marriage, and he was bound by them. It was beside the point that he'd made that deal only because he couldn't imagine ever being seriously attracted to her.

And he still couldn't, he reminded himself. Not really. Eve was gorgeous, yes, but she was also as cold and hard as the gemstones he worked with every day.

Of course, when he'd promised to leave her strictly alone, he hadn't expected that they'd be sharing a bed, no matter how accidentally or unwillingly. And he hadn't anticipated that steamy kiss at the airport, either. If she hadn't flung herself into his arms like that, he might not have ever wondered if the glacier he'd married might be perched atop a volcano.

Now, just thinking about that kiss made his palms ache to hold her again.

He punched his pillow again, irritably, and noticed that the suite had gone totally silent. Eve was holding her breath.

But then, David realized, so was he.

David was floating on a silken cloud that smelled faintly of lilacs when he was rudely awakened by the sound of his name.

He opened his eyes and, finding himself nose to nose with Eve, lay very still for a moment to take stock of the situation. The blanket barricade was no longer in the center of the bed; it seemed to have been pushed into a heap near the footboard. The silken, lilac-scented cloud under his cheek was her hair. Quite unintentionally, he had anchored her to the bed so she couldn't even turn her head. No wonder she'd sounded as if her teeth were clenched; they probably were.

I'm a dead man, he thought.

"If you don't mind," Eve said coldly.

David raised his head and she pulled free, turned to look at the bedside clock, and shrieked. The sound scratched his nerves. "Do you always wake up in this kind of mood?" he asked irritably.

"Only when I oversleep. But I don't see how it can possibly be so late, because I set the alarm clock for seven."

He looked around her at the clock on her bedside table, which announced that it was a few minutes past nine. He stretched out a hand for his wristwatch. "Maybe it's fast."

She was fiddling with the clock. "It's not working," she said in disbelief. "The alarm, I mean. I can't believe it—this hotel takes pride in fixing things almost before they break."

"Maybe nobody's reported it. An alarm clock in the bridal suite—it could have been out of commission for months."

"I don't see how it could escape notice."

"Easily, my dear. You see—"

"Don't start with the eyebrows again," Eve said irritably. "You don't have to explain to me why brides and grooms like to sleep late. I only meant that even they must have planes to catch sometimes."

"If they're smart, they schedule all flights for after noon." He rolled out of bed. "Besides, you did say you didn't want to look haggard this morning, so an extra couple of hours of sleep—"

"Well, I'm *feeling* haggard." She pulled open the

closet door and ripped the plastic garment bag off her new dress. "We'll have to hurry."

"What's the point? We're already so late it won't make any difference."

But she'd vanished into the bathroom and apparently didn't hear.

They'd lingered over the Chateaubriand the previous evening instead of packing, so while David waited, he pulled his suitcases out of the closet and began to empty the drawers. Eve reappeared, a mascara brush in one hand and his pajamas in the other. "Here," she said. "Thanks for the loan. And don't look at me like that. Of course I know I should return them fresh and clean, but I don't have room for extras in my tote bag."

David, beginning to feel more than a little contrary himself, dumped the pajamas atop the pile of shirts in his suitcase. "Don't forget your lace nightie. What did you do with it, anyway? I haven't seen it since Saturday night."

"Surely you don't think that's an accident. I was trying to leave it behind." She pulled open a drawer and tossed the frothy white negligee at him. "Here—you want it, you pack it."

He tossed it back. "Use the box it came in. If you leave it, the maids will probably take it straight to the hotel manager, and the staff at Birmingham on State wouldn't be amused."

"How would they know I don't have it anymore? I wasn't planning to wear it next time I invite them all to tea."

"Because the manager would probably bring it to you at the store."

"Good point. She'd do exactly that." Eve shoved the negligee ruthlessly into a side pocket of her tote bag.

The lace, David noticed, was so flimsy that it compressed to almost nothing. "What are we doing with the luggage?" he asked. "I don't fancy walking into the store dragging a couple of suitcases."

"I suppose we could leave it all in the checkroom down in the lobby and pick it up after work." Eve shivered. "No, on second thought, I'd just as soon not show my face in this hotel again for a while. We'll have to run out to my apartment and drop it off. Are you going to be ready soon? I don't want to be any later than we have to be."

"I suppose that rules out breakfast," David muttered. "But at least we don't have to waste a precious few minutes this morning rumpling up the bed."

Birmingham on State had been open for almost an hour by the time their cab pulled up in front. Eve looked at her watch, then at a pair of women who had just come out of the store carrying small pastel-peach shopping bags, and sighed. "We've definitely got to work out a better system for the mornings. I don't think I can handle having customers leaving before I arrive."

"If you're thinking of posting a schedule on the refrigerator door, I object." David offered a hand to help her out of the cab. "And I'm sure no alarm clock that belongs to you would dare go off late, so it shouldn't be a problem from here on out."

"Just because I like things to do what they're supposed to, David—"

He pulled open the door and leaned closer to whisper, "Smile, darling, we have an audience."

Eve had already noticed that every employee of Birmingham on State seemed to have found an excuse to congregate in the main showroom. As they came in, she noted, heads turned and a couple of people discreetly checked their watches.

Eve felt like reminding them of the hundreds of mornings when she had been the first to arrive. But a defensive attitude wasn't very dignified—and in any case she had nothing to be defensive about. Her job had never required her to punch a time clock, because she worked whatever hours were necessary to get the job done.

"Good morning," she said, doing her best to feign cheerfulness. "How nice of you all to make a point of greeting us." She started across the showroom toward her office at the back.

David caught up with her in two steps and put a hand on her shoulder. She swung around and he brushed a kiss across her lips. "I'll be in my workroom concentrating on Mrs. Morgan's necklace, darling."

Eve gave him her most stunning smile, but under her breath she said, "I'll remember that in the unlikely event I discover I can't live without you."

From the corner of her eye she saw one of the male salesclerks pull a bill from his money clip and hand it to the woman standing next to him. *That's odd. Oh— they're probably still taking up a collection to pay for that incredible waste of lace. Which reminds me...*

She raised her voice. "I want to thank you all for the gift. It's lovely."

"It certainly is," David chimed in. "I'll be writing each and every one of you a personal thank-you note, of course, for your thoughtfulness in giving Eve something that meant so much to me. But in the meantime—"

Eve could feel her skin flaming.

"It was a wonderful choice," David went on.

She smiled at him and said through gritted teeth, "Will you knock it off?"

He leaned in as if to nuzzle her ear and whispered, "I suppose you'd think I was being crude if I told them it spent the greater part of our wedding night on the floor."

Even though it's the precise, absolute truth.

Eve glared at him with what she hoped looked like nothing more than fond, if exasperated, embarrassment, and once more started for her office.

But she stopped short as she came near it—for lounging in the doorway, where he had a sidelong view of the showroom, was Travis Tate.

Eve caught her breath. "You're still in Chicago?" She caught herself just a moment too late and tried to sound casual. "I thought you'd have gone on to your next stop by now."

His eyes gleamed. "So you're still keeping track of my schedule. Normally I would have moved on, of course. But Henry was too busy to see me last week."

"Then perhaps you'd better go up to see him now." She brushed past him and leaned over her desk to look at the mail lying there.

He stopped just inside her office, watching her closely. "I have seen him. But it was so unusual, you not being here at this time of morning, that I decided to hang around for a bit to see what happened next. That was quite an interesting show, Eve darling. I suppose I wasn't really surprised."

She didn't look up. "You mean after seeing David and me at the airport?"

"Oh, no. I mean after hearing the whispers in the industry that Henry was thinking about retiring. What a nice little package it all makes…for your new husband, at least. But, Eve—sweet Eve—I'm shocked, my dear, really I am. For a woman who made so much fuss about morals to sell yourself so cheaply—''

David spoke from the doorway. ''Is this man bothering you, Eve?''

''No. He's just on his way out.''

Travis smiled coldly. ''So he's the possessive sort, too, this new husband of yours. But then that's really no surprise, either. For someone who's never had anything before, he's suddenly got a lot to lose if he doesn't keep his bride happy. Or possibly the word I'm looking for, instead of happy, is *deluded.* I wonder which it will turn out to be.'' He gave a mocking salute as he turned toward the door.

David stepped aside to let him pass.

Eve tried, without much success, to keep her hands from trembling. As soon as Travis was out of earshot, she said, ''I don't know why you had to rush in like that. I didn't need to be protected from him.''

''Is that what it looked like I was trying to do? Throw you a life preserver?'' David sounded only mildly interested. ''Too bad he didn't stick around long enough to be introduced. Such a charming guy he appears to be. Henry wants to talk to both of us—over breakfast.''

''Whose idea was that, I wonder.'' She didn't intend it to be a question.

''The breakfast part was mine, of course. He seemed quite touched when I told him we…uh…had other priorities besides food this morning.''

Eve's jaw dropped. ''You didn't tell him that,'' she accused.

''Tell him what? That we were too busy making love to get out of bed on time? I don't see why you should be shocked. That's the idea you obviously want him to get.''

''I didn't plan to lie to him about it!''

''You just intend to let him draw his own conclusions—mistaken though they may be.''

''There's a big difference, David.''

''Yes, there is—which is why I didn't tell him anything of the sort. It's interesting, however, to contemplate where your mind leaped right away. But Henry's waiting for us at the front door, so we'll have to take up that discussion later.''

Much later, Eve thought in chagrin. *Like in some future lifetime, if I have anything to say about it.* What had possessed her to jump to that conclusion—and, worse, to let him know it?

''So tell me about the man who was just here,'' David said.

Eve fought off a shiver. ''There's nothing to tell. He's just like those dozen live-in lovers you've supposedly had—nobody worth worrying about.''

''Perhaps it hasn't occurred to you that's why I'm worried,'' David murmured.

Henry was standing beside the display case closest to the front door, talking to a salesclerk. Eve saw him slide his wallet into his pocket just as the clerk tucked a bill into an envelope. ''I'll take the first day next week that's open,'' he said. Turning, he grinned at Eve and David. ''Breakfast,'' he said. He rubbed his hands together and reached for his cane, lying atop the display case. ''A marvelous idea. I didn't manage any myself this morning.''

As they walked down the street to Henry's favorite tavern, Eve was frowning. ''What was that all about, Henry? You don't normally hand out cash to the employees.''

Henry blinked innocently at her. "I beg your pardon, my dear?"

Eve could almost see the glint of a halo above his left ear, and she braced herself.

David took her arm. "I believe it's called an office pool, sweetheart. Everybody pitches in a few bucks and chooses a possible outcome, and the one who comes closest to what actually happens collects the pot."

"I know what a pool is," she said crossly. "But the World Series is over, and the basketball season's hardly started."

"There are more things to bet on than sports," David murmured. "I'd guess, myself, that it has something to do with how everyone's eyes went to the clock a few minutes ago when we walked in."

Eve's jaw dropped and she swung around to face her grandfather. "You were actually betting on when we'd get to work today?"

"Not this morning," Henry said easily. "But as time went on and you still didn't show up, there was some speculation about how long it might take you to get back on your regular schedule. So the winner of the pool is the one who chooses the day you actually manage to walk in on time. Of course now that you know about it, it's hardly a fair bet anymore, so I suppose we'll have to call it off."

"You do that," Eve said. "Because the winner will be whoever was lucky enough to draw tomorrow."

Henry nodded gently, but he didn't answer. At the tavern, he headed automatically for his favorite booth and settled himself comfortably in the center of one of the red-vinyl benches.

Eve reluctantly took the other side, sliding as far as she could to leave room for David beside her. The booths were small and despite the fact that she was pressed against the wall, she could feel the warmth of him next to her and the brush of pin-striped wool against her silky stocking as their knees bumped.

Belatedly, Henry seemed to notice the lack of space. "Would you rather have a table? We could move."

David didn't answer, just looked at Eve as if he was curious whether she'd grab at the opportunity to escape.

She was darned if she'd admit that being this close to him bothered her. "Oh, no, I just love being squashed in the corner like this. It makes me feel secure and protected. What did you want to talk to us about, Henry?"

Henry waved a waitress over. "The advertising campaign, mainly. I thought about it a lot over the weekend and it seems to me that we need to have a meeting with the team that came up with this new idea before we agree to proceed."

"But I've already given preliminary approval," Eve objected.

"That was before you had time to look everything over," David said. "So you were really just acknowledging that you were given the materials."

She gave him a sideways look. "I should have known you had a hand in this."

"I didn't arrange this, Eve. I just pointed out that without something more formal, there isn't any deal. Birmingham on State isn't committed to going ahead—not yet."

"And by *something more formal,* you mean your approval, I suppose?"

Henry intervened. "I believe we need to hear from them why they think they've been so clever, and exactly why they expect the campaign will be well-received. It'll only work if we all believe in it, you know."

"I don't think that's true," Eve protested. "We've had campaigns before that I wasn't entirely sold on, and—"

"And maybe there were better ones which were passed over because you didn't object," David said. "I think that's fair, Henry. A meeting, that's all. If they can convince me, I'll withdraw my objections."

"Fine," Eve said. "I'll set one up. Now if that's all we need to discuss, I'm going back to work."

She expected an argument, but David slid silently out of the booth so she could stand. As she crossed the tavern, she heard him tell Henry earnestly, "She's just a little cranky when she doesn't have breakfast."

The building supervisor had been in the lobby that morning when they'd dropped off their luggage, so they'd left it with him instead of going upstairs. When Eve unlocked the door of her apartment that evening, she noticed that her hand was trembling just a little. But that was silly, she thought. They'd shared much closer quarters than this over the weekend. She should be relieved to be home. At least in the apartment they weren't confined to a single room together, and there were no doormen or housekeeping staff or hotel managers keeping a supposedly helpful eye out for them.

But somehow this felt like an even bigger change. The hotel suite, by its very nature, had been a temporary arrangement. Having David move into her apartment felt much more permanent somehow. Much more momentous.

She stepped around the suitcases, which the supervisor had brought upstairs and piled just inside the door. "You'll need the extra key," she said. "It's in the drawer of the hall table. I'm sure we won't be commuting together every day.''

David didn't answer. She glanced up to see that he was checking out the surroundings, and almost automatically she looked around herself. Though she'd lived in the apartment for more than two years, it seemed she, too, was seeing it for the first time.

A wide hallway stretched as far as she could see, bending out of sight to set the bedroom wing off from the more public areas. All along one side of the hallway were bookshelves; opposite the shelves hung a collection of framed photographs. To her left lay an open kitchen. Off to the right, a high archway led into a large living room. Airy and sunny in the daytime, it was always far less cozy with darkness closing in. With the push of a button, Eve ignited the gas log in the fireplace and sank down on the leather couch in front of the blaze.

''It makes sense, though,'' David said. ''Using one cab instead of two, I mean. Or do you usually take your car?''

''And try to park it downtown? This isn't a town for drivers.''

He nodded. ''That's why I sold my car instead of driving it out here. I figured if I was wrong, I could always buy another one.''

''Good decision. Even in the apartment complex, parking spaces are at a premium.'' She looked up at him, still standing just inside the archway.

The apartment was quite a lot larger than the suite had been, but somehow it didn't feel much bigger. She hadn't anticipated that David would somehow seem to take up the entire space. He'd said something about a house—well, it was already obvious to Eve that they were definitely going to have to think about that soon.

And they'd be looking for a big house, with plenty of rooms for privacy.

"I'll unpack later," she said. "For right now I'm just going to sit still and recuperate. The guest room's down the hall on the right."

David didn't move. "Good. Since you're just going to be sitting there, you can tell me about Travis Tate. One of the salesclerks told me his name."

She went still, every muscle absolutely motionless. Under the pressures of the day, she'd almost forgotten the incident this morning.

After a long moment, David said, "At least I assume he's one of the things you're recuperating from."

Eve jumped to her feet.

David hadn't moved, but he seemed to be blocking the door anyway. "Are you planning to walk out on me?"

"I'm not staying here to be cross-examined, that's for sure. I haven't asked you for details about the women in your life." Too late, when she saw how his eyes narrowed, Eve realized what she'd admitted. She hadn't succeeded in putting him in his place, as she'd intended to do. She'd only confirmed his suspicions.

"So he *is* important," David said softly.

She sat down again almost in slow motion, sinking onto the very end of the couch. She'd like to huddle against the overstuffed arm for protection, but she knew it wouldn't do any good.

He was looking at her levelly. There was no judgment in his gaze, but there wasn't much flexibility, either. He wasn't going to give up.

"He was important," she admitted. "Once." A real gentleman, she thought, would take her word for it and stop right there.

But obviously David wasn't feeling chivalrous this evening, for he asked, "He isn't important now?"

She shook her head. "No. Not for several months."

"What happened?"

"Why should it matter? I told you it's over, and you can take my word for it. So that's all there is to say."

"It matters," David said gently, "because the gentleman doesn't seem to agree with you that it's over."

She caught her lower lip between her teeth.

"Who is he? What does he do?"

She sighed. "He's a sales representative for a gem broker. He calls on Henry once a month or so."

"So that's why he was at the store. What about the airport?"

"He works out of New York City, so he travels a lot."

"And I suppose the poor guy gets lonely."

She heard the irony in his voice, but she ignored it. "Moving from hotel to hotel all the time can get to be pretty boring."

"So he was looking for companionship…"

"We started seeing each other, whenever he was in town. We weren't dating, it was just friendship. But—"

"But then you fell in love with him."

"Yes." She had no reason to be ashamed of it, after all. "And in case you're wondering, he fell in love with me, too."

David shifted in his chair. "I see. It appears we have all the necessary ingredients for a fairy tale. So let's see, what could have happened to make you end up married to me instead? I've got it. Henry objected because Travis didn't fit in with his plans for the store."

"Henry didn't know about it."

David's eyebrows lifted as if he had his doubts about that.

Eve fought down a childish desire to get a razor and shave them off.

"Then if the breakup wasn't Henry's doing, what was the obstacle that derailed the romance?"

"We hadn't intended it to be a romance," Eve pointed out.

"But despite your good intentions, your feelings overcame you. That often happens."

"Does it?" Her voice felt lifeless. "I wouldn't know."

"Really? I thought every teenager had to listen to that bit of cosmic wisdom about never dating anyone who you wouldn't consider marrying, because these things have a habit of getting out of control. In my case, it was my father, and he didn't phrase it exactly that way. But surely your mother—"

Eve shook her head. "My mother never told me anything about dating. She left my father when I was five, and I saw her only rarely after that."

He looked as if she'd kicked him. "I'm sorry, Eve. I didn't know that."

"How could you have, any more than I could know about your mother dying? The divorce wasn't a secret, of course, but not very many people know why she left."

"Why?" he asked gently.

She didn't look at him. "She broke up her marriage because she stopped caring about my father and fell in love with another man, and so she went off to seek her happiness."

"Leaving you with half a family. At least that explains why you never heard the standard lectures, and even why the idea of an arranged marriage didn't turn you off.''

Eve shrugged. "I suppose so. My parents were in love—but it didn't matter much in the end.''

"Let's get back to Travis and why you didn't marry him.''

The man was like a bulldog; he simply didn't let go of anything. "Because I couldn't.''

"Let me guess.'' David paced the living room. "I can think of three reasons, off the top of my head.'' He ticked them off on his fingers. "He's not the marrying kind, or he's gay, or he's already married. I'd have to put my money on him having a little wife tucked quietly away somewhere.''

"She wasn't tucked away.''

For the first time he looked as if she'd surprised him. "You knew he was married? Honey, if you mess around with a guy who already has a wife, you shouldn't be surprised if he goes back to her.''

"He didn't. I mean… Must you twist this all around and make it sound so sordid?''

"If you don't want me to put my own interpretation on it, quit stalling and tell me what happened.''

"All right!'' She took a deep breath. "I didn't know he was married. At first, when we were just friends, there was no reason for him to tell me. Anyway, they were separated—''

"Of course they were.''

"I don't know why you sound so suspicious, David. It happens all the time.''

"Exactly. So often that nobody even thinks much about it anymore when a marriage breaks up. So why didn't he get a divorce and marry you?''

"He would have. But I couldn't let him, because…''

Her voice sank. It hurt to say this, to expose her feelings. "Because he has two little girls. They're six and three."

David whistled. "And you thought of your own childhood, and you couldn't do the same thing to them that your mother's lover did to you."

She nodded. The gesture felt jerky. "I told him he had to go back and make it work, for the sake of the children."

"Something of a miscalculation on Mr. Tate's part, I'd say."

"What do you mean?"

"No doubt he wasn't one of the elite few who'd heard about your mother, or he'd have known better than to let you find out about the kids till he was certain of you."

Eve jumped up. "Stop it!"

"I thought you said he wasn't important anymore, Eve."

"That doesn't mean I'm going to let you say nasty things about him. How would you know anything about it? He didn't set out to hurt anybody. He was caught up in circumstances beyond his control, the same way I was. There was nothing else I could do. And I'm not going to talk about it anymore. The subject is closed, understand? It's finished." She stepped around him and went down the hall to her bedroom. She felt like going straight on—down the fire escape, across the city, past the Mississippi River and the Rocky Mountains....

How were they ever going to make this work?

Not a house, she told herself. *No house we could buy would possibly be big enough. We need to shop for a subdivision.*

CHAPTER SIX

THE guest room was small, and though she'd obviously tried to make him feel welcome, David thought the room still felt more like an office than a bedroom. The desk had been hastily pushed aside to open up the space; he could see the indentations in the carpet where it used to stand, almost in the center of the room. Half of the closet was taken up with neatly marked files and boxes, and the narrow bed was piled with pillows so it could function more like a couch. A single small chest served to hold a printer as well as a visitor's belongings.

It was apparent to David that Eve didn't have overnight guests very often. *Or if she does,* a little voice in the back of his brain suggested, *they don't use the guest room.*

If, for instance, Travis Tate had come to visit…

Knock it off, David ordered himself. What difference did it make if he had? It was none of his business. Eve had told him the relationship was over, and he had no reason to doubt her sincerity. The pain in her voice had made it obvious that she had not made her decision lightly but only after agonizing consideration.

Still…the whole story didn't quite hang together.

He stacked the frivolous pillows in a corner, turned off the lights, and tried to get comfortable in the narrow bed. Folding his arms under his head and staring at the ceiling, he thought about what she'd told him.

It was an old story, of course. A married man and a vulnerable woman who'd fallen for the line he'd spun for her. Only most women wouldn't have called it quits where Eve had. She hadn't fallen into the trap of thinking that her boyfriend's little girls would automatically be better off if their quarreling parents split. Of course, with her history, she'd known better. She'd been hurt too badly herself as a child to deliberately cause the same kind of anguish for a couple of other little girls.

I did the only thing I could, she'd told him, and the pain in her voice convinced him she'd believed what she was saying.

But no matter what she believed, it simply wasn't true, and now David knew what had been niggling at him. There were other options—a middle ground that lay between breaking up a family and entirely giving up the man she loved. Why—for instance—had she never considered simply waiting till Travis Tate's children were grown? If she cared so much for him, surely that possibility should have occurred to her.

Or maybe it did, David thought, *and she decided it was too long to wait.*

The children were very young, of course—six and three, had she said?—and it would have been a long wait indeed. But surely, if she was really as serious about Travis as she thought she was, she'd have at least thought about it. And considering how high and mighty her reasons were, even a fifteen-year wait—until the younger child went to college—surely wouldn't have seemed too long.

If Eve really believed that she loved Travis and that she would never care for anyone else, why hadn't she just hunkered down to tough it out? And why, when Henry suggested she make a practical marriage instead, hadn't she told him to take a flying leap into Lake Michigan?

Certainly not because she was impatient or afraid of long-term promises—because instead of waiting for the man she loved, she'd chosen to contract a marriage of convenience. A marriage she said she intended to last forever.

She'd thought she was being completely honest, he was convinced of that. But was she really telling the whole truth? Did she even know what she intended? Was it possible that subconsciously, buried so deeply that even she didn't know it, Eve intended this marriage as a stop-gap measure, nothing more than a way to keep Henry happy and herself occupied until Travis Tate would be free of his responsibilities?

I have my reasons, she'd said, *for wanting the protection of a wedding ring, without emotional entanglements...*

The words rang hollow in his mind.

David rolled over, wincing at the ache in the small of his back from a too soft mattress. But he knew it wasn't just the narrow bed that was making him uncomfortable.

He'd taken her at her word. He'd bet his future on her promise.

Had he been a fool to put so much faith in what she said?

The mechanical tick-tick-tick of the wall clock in the guest room wore on David's nerves like the steady dripping of water. At least there was no worry about him oversleeping, he thought wryly. Under that form of torture, there was no question of sleeping at all.

He took the clock off the wall and removed the batteries. But the resulting dead silence was no more conducive to rest. No wonder Eve liked this apartment building, he thought. The walls were so thick that it seemed they were alone in the universe.

Not exactly a comforting image, Elliot.

He might as well get up and do something. There were a couple of designs that had been nagging at him. The necklace he was supposed to be making out of the nuggets from Mrs. Morgan's ring collection, for instance. It hadn't quite come together in his mind yet—and perhaps making a few sketches, trying out a few ideas, would take his mind off Eve, as well.

His hand closed on the knob of the middle desk drawer, but he stopped there. The idea of opening it, even to look for a blank piece of paper, made him uncomfortable—as if he'd be violating her privacy. Stupid, really, he told himself. He was certain that she'd removed any personal items which had been inside. It wasn't as if he was likely to find passionate love letters from Travis Tate.

But, shaking his head at his own hesitation, he tiptoed down the hallway toward where he'd left his briefcase, on the table by the front door. Just around the bend in the hallway, he realized that Eve, too, must be awake, because light streamed from the kitchen doorway even though he was certain he'd turned it off.

She was sitting at the island counter, a slice of cold pizza in one hand and a plate in front of her.

She's such a perfect lady she won't even eat cold pizza without putting it on a plate.

"I hope you like pepperoni," he said. "I would have asked before I ordered, but you seemed to be having such a good time sulking that I didn't want to interrupt."

She swung around, and a plaid napkin slid off her lap and onto the floor. "I was not sulking."

He wondered if she'd bought the voluminous granny

nightie with him in mind, or if it was her usual choice
of nightwear. He guessed that the manufacturer had
started with roughly an acre of some plain white fabric,
then gathered and ruffled and fancy-stitched it together
until it was at least four layers thick everywhere he
looked, and it actually almost fit her.

What the garment didn't do, despite its magnitude,
was to hide her slender frame. She should have been lost
among the bulky folds—which no doubt had been her
intention. Instead the pleats and gathers served to em-
phasize the curves that lay beneath. The narrow cuffs
dipped intriguingly over the back of her hands, display-
ing a glimpse of wrist as she put her pizza down on the
plate. The small round collar simply made the arch of
her throat more artistic. And the hem rustled invitingly
as she moved, calling attention to the slim bare foot that
peeked out under it.

In its own way, the gown was even more interesting
than the white lace confection delivered to the honeymoon suite on their wedding night. In a completely different way, of course—because the negligee had enticed
by revealing, but this nightgown left everything to the
imagination.

And his imagination, David realized, was a pretty
powerful force. He was having no trouble whatsoever
filling in the gaps between the few inches of flesh he
could see.

Time for a distraction, Elliot.

"Is that the last of the pizza?" he asked.

Eve shook her head. "No, there's more. This is all I
want."

His arm brushed her shoulder as he opened the refrigerator, and he felt her involuntary shiver. For an instant,
he was almost annoyed. Did she honestly think she was

in danger from him? That the fact they were dressed for bed meant he couldn't think of anything else?

"Thanks for ordering the pizza," she said without looking at him.

"I looked around the kitchen first. The choices were pretty slim."

"I know. The cleaning service will restock tomorrow, so if there's anything you want them to get, put it on the list." She pointed at the refrigerator door where a scribbled page was tacked up by a magnet. "I'm going back to bed. What about you? I mean—" She stopped and turned pink.

As if I'd be expecting an invitation to join her, David thought. "I think I'll work for a while."

She slid off the kitchen stool, and the sway of the voluminous gown showed off an ankle. "See you in the morning, then."

She'd left her pizza sitting on the plate, she'd been in such a hurry to get away. He sat down and thoughtfully bit into the thick, chewy crust as he reached for a pencil and memo pad which lay on the counter. His hand began to move, sketching a lacy web of a necklace.

Then it hit him. Eve hadn't been shuddering in distaste. And she hadn't ducked out of the room in fear, either. At least, she wasn't afraid for the usual reasons. David wasn't a threat to her safety; he was a threat to her beliefs—and at some level she knew it.

She obviously believed that she still loved Travis Tate. And perhaps she did, in a way. Perhaps she always would.

But despite her conviction—despite her determination to remain true to the man she couldn't have—she had already moved on. She had left Travis behind when she ended their affair. When she had decided not to wait for him, she had, without even knowing it, freed herself for other possibilities. Whether she realized it or not, the glacier was beginning to thaw and break up. She could deny it, but she couldn't make it less true—she was vulnerable.

The evidence was that shiver of hers. It had been one of awareness. Awareness of David—of the man she had married.

Or was he only kidding himself? Was he letting his desires get in the way of good sense?

Because there was no denying anymore that he found her desirable. Or that he was intrigued by the challenge she presented. Heating up the glacier—now that would be a job worth undertaking.

He looked down at the memo pad and realized that he hadn't been drawing a necklace at all. Left to itself while his mind wandered, his hand had sketched the pattern that had been stitched with bright-colored thread and ribbon around the top of her nightgown. Scallops and frills and knots formed a complicated motif that he hadn't even consciously noticed.

It had apparently imprinted itself on his brain. Just as Eve seemed to have done.

Eve was awake before her alarm went off, largely because of a dream that she'd been wrapped like a mummy and buried in a hot, airless pyramid. It was a perfectly logical—though subconscious—interpretation, she realized as soon as she opened her eyes. Her quilted comforter was pulled over her head, and the substantial folds of her nightgown had swaddled 'round her as she tossed and turned through the night, restricting her movements till she had trouble unwrapping herself enough to get out of bed.

She found a dash of black humor in the idea that if she couldn't break free by herself she could always call for David to rescue her. After all, since he was the reason she was in the predicament in the first place, he might as well help her out of it. If it hadn't been for him, she'd have never looked twice at a nightgown that could double as a circus tent.

Once free, she eyed the crumpled cotton gown in the mirror with distaste. It hadn't been quite the success she'd hoped. Though it had gotten exactly the reaction she'd expected from David—the look he'd given her last night said quite clearly that Grandma Moses would have been more inviting—the gown hadn't made her feel quite as secure as she'd expected it would. Being swathed in that much fabric should have been like wearing chain mail. Instead, she'd felt as if she was wrapped in waxed paper. Fortunately, David hadn't bothered to look—but still…

There was nothing in the closet she wanted to wear. Finally she seized a dress from the basket that was awaiting the attentions of the cleaning crew and, pulling a terry robe over her lacy underthings, took it to the kitchen to press.

David was nowhere in sight, but the coffeepot was sighing as it finished the cycle. Eve poured herself a cup and was testing the iron when he walked in, still settling his tie.

"This is a switch," she said. "You'll actually have time for breakfast while I get dressed."

"Yeah, as long as I want leftover pizza."

She wielded the iron expertly across the collar of the dress. "Now who's being grumpy? You look as if you didn't sleep at all."

"I didn't, much. I was thinking."

Eve kept her gaze on the pleated back of the dress. "You'll notice that I'm not asking what you were thinking about."

"Doesn't matter, because I'm going to tell you anyway. I was thinking about you and Travis Tate."

She set the iron down with a thump. "If the next thing out of your mouth is to demand the details, forget it. It's none of your business and I'm not about to gratify your lecherous curiosity."

"That's all right. There's nothing else I need to know. You've already told me you had a full-fledged affair with him."

Eve stared at him, open-mouthed. "I don't remember saying anything of the kind."

"You admitted there were details," he said, sounding impatient. "Pretty juicy ones, too, it sounds like, or you wouldn't object to talking about them."

"I'm not even going to dignify that with a comment, David."

"And as a result of that affair, you've decided that you're going to live out the rest of your life without any further intimate contact. If you can't have Travis, you won't have anybody."

"What about it?" She picked up the iron again.

"You can't do it." His voice was calm and level.

"If you think you're going to issue orders to me—" Eve remembered the iron and yanked it away from a lacy frill barely a moment before it would have started to melt.

"I'm not doing anything of the kind. I'm just making a simple statement of fact. You can't do it."

"You seriously don't think I can go the rest of my life without a man in my bed?"

"That's right. I don't."

She stared at him, honestly curious. "Why?"

"You may be in shock now, because of what happened with Travis. But sooner or later the urges are going to come back. Only someone who doesn't know what she's missing could turn her back on physical gratification."

"Obviously you don't understand women." She shook out the dress and put the finishing touches on the cuffs. "You know, that's the major problem with men—they assume that women feel the same way they do. Because you're feeling deprived, you assume that I must be, too."

"Maybe not at the moment, but you will be."

"I'll let you know if it happens," Eve said dryly. "Don't hold your breath in the meantime. Though, come to think of it, what business is it of yours?"

"Plenty, I'd say, because whenever you give up the frigid act, I'm likely to get caught in the crossfire."

"I suppose you think I'll be overcome with a fit of desire someday and I'll pick up the first stranger I run into on the street? Or are you hoping I'll attack you some night because I'm starving for attention? In your dreams, David. I'm completely immune."

His voice was silky. "You're sure of that?"

She had turned to unplug the iron, and so she didn't see him move until he was beside her. He took the iron out of her hand, setting it aside and in the same motion sweeping her into his arms and molding her against his body.

The heat of him seemed to turn the heavy terry cloth of her robe into plastic wrap that melted and clung and glued her to him. *Slap him,* her brain ordered. But her hand refused to move.

The first time he'd kissed her, in the airport, had been

hot and demanding—but that had been entirely her fault; she'd asked for it. The second time, at their wedding, he'd been a little more restrained—but again it had been a deliberate performance, with an attentive audience.

This kiss was pure, steamy sensuality—teasing, tantalizing, and seductive. He tasted her slowly, exploring her mouth with a gentleness that made her ache, then turning his attention to her earlobe and finally her throat, his lips moving slowly down to the shadowed valley where the robe's neckline gaped, to brush the lacy edge of her bra.

Eve gasped. She felt as if she was caught in a fire; each breath of air was hot and thick and painful. But the worst thing of all, she realized hazily when he stopped kissing her, was that he hadn't used an ounce of force. At the end, he'd hardly been holding her at all. He hadn't needed to, for she'd been pressing herself against him instead.

"Still feeling immune?" His voice had a rough edge, as if he was having a little trouble breathing himself.

"All I feel at the moment," Eve managed to say, "is a strong desire to sink a carving knife into your ribs."

A slow smile lit his eyes. "It would be such a shame to be stabbed over a single kiss," he murmured. "*Two,* on the other hand…" He stretched out one arm as if to pull her close again.

Eve ducked away. "Don't you dare!"

David folded his arms across his chest and leaned against the sink. "I don't have to, because I've already made my point. You're a long way from being immune, Eve, and now you know it. The truth is, sooner or later you're going to regret what you're missing."

"So I suppose you think I should have an affair with you."

He shook his head.

Eve felt an odd twinge deep inside.

"Married people can't have an affair. Not with each other."

Eve's breath came back with a rush. *Well, that's a relief.*

"But I think you should sleep with me," he went on. "It makes perfect sense. You're happy, I'm happy, Henry's happy—"

"I suppose two out of three wouldn't be a bad percentage," Eve said coolly. "But you've overlooked something, David. You agreed to the conditions, and you're not changing the rules now."

"You're right. I'm not."

Warily, Eve looked him over.

"I think it's up to you to change them," David said easily. "Whenever you decide to, I'll be right here."

"I hope you enjoy waiting, because I don't feel any obligation to make your life easier, Elliot. We had an agreement. It's not my fault you've fallen in lust."

"Oh, that's cute."

"Well, you'd better not insult me by saying it's anything more than lust. Because the truth is, any woman who walked by right now would satisfy your urges. Henry got that much right, at least, when he arranged—" She caught a glimpse of the bright green numbers on the front of the microwave and broke off suddenly. "Oh, no!"

"What?" David looked around.

She pointed at the digital clock. "We're going to be late. *Again.*"

She had married a louse, Eve told herself. There was simply no other way to put it, for what else could you call a guy who agreed to a perfectly reasonable, straight-forward bargain and then went back on his word?

Furthermore, he wasn't even giving her the satisfaction she should have gotten from turning him down. Instead of acting disgruntled, or offended, or even disappointed, David seemed not to have noticed that she'd utterly and completely refused to consider his proposition. He chatted gently all the way across the Loop in the cab, and though she tried to avoid him, he took her arm as they walked across the sidewalk to the main entrance of Birmingham on State. "Careful, Eve," he murmured. "You might accidentally give me the idea that my mere touch bothers you." He pulled the door open for her.

She smiled up at him with clenched teeth. "It does—just not in the way you'd like to think."

The crowd waiting for them inside the store was only slightly smaller than it had been yesterday. Henry was in the midst of it, arranging a new necklace in one of the display cases. He paused to look ostentatiously at his wristwatch. "Ah, children. Only thirty minutes late today, I see."

"Sorry to disappoint you, Henry," David said. "I told Eve that since you all wouldn't be expecting us for another hour at least, we might as well—"

She stepped on his foot, hard.

David winced, but he didn't pause. "—finish the deeply philosophical discussion we were having."

Eve thought he sounded positively sanctimonious—just like Henry did when he was lying a blue streak. A couple of staff members obviously agreed, for they chuckled as if enjoying the joke.

The sharp knife in the ribs she'd threatened him with, Eve thought grimly, was far too good for him.

Refusing to look at David, she held her head high and cast a glance over the crowd, catching a speculative gleam in Henry's eyes. He looked quite pleased with himself.

And no wonder, Eve thought. Though Henry couldn't possibly know that David was turning out to be everything the old man had hoped for, he obviously had his suspicions. It was almost a shame that he was going to be disappointed anyway.

Henry hadn't asked her for promises, but he'd never made any secret of his hopes that this marriage would produce an heir for the business he had nurtured and cherished and protected. Guilt flickered through her at the thought of how let down he would ultimately be when he found out that was never going to happen.

But her pang of guilt was quickly replaced by something little short of indignation. David himself had said the whole idea was medieval, back when she'd first enlightened him about Henry's hopes and dreams. He'd been startled that Eve had agreed to the old man's plan, and relieved when she'd laid out her terms.

Yet now he had fallen neatly in with Henry's plans, leaving Eve to stand alone. Very much alone.

What really annoyed Eve was how little it had apparently taken to change his mind. As far as she could see, just because she was right in front of him—and theoretically available—David was suddenly quite willing to take advantage of the situation.

Men, she growled to herself. The whole thing was simply unfair.

"It's my turn to buy breakfast, Henry," David offered cheerfully. "I've got some ideas I want to run past you."

Henry nodded and closed the display case.

As the two men approached the front door, Eve stepped into their path. "Excuse me."

"Are you feeling left out, sweetheart?" David asked cheerfully. "Sorry I didn't ask you to come along, but since you've got this thing about breakfast—"

Eve gritted her teeth. It was getting to be a habit. "No, thank you," she said politely. "I just wanted to remind you both that we've got a meeting with the ad agency later this morning."

"Did you set it up for here or at their office?" Henry asked.

"There. It seemed more sensible than asking them to bring everything and everyone to the store."

Henry nodded. "We'll be back in plenty of time." He turned to David. "How are you coming along with that necklace of Mrs. Morgan's?"

"Quite well, I think." David's voice faded as the two men went out. "It's all thanks to Eve, because she presented me with a true inspiration last night."

Much more of that, Eve thought irritably, *and I'll* inspire *him all right.* Exactly what kind of tale was he going to tell Henry now—all about their supposed pillow talk?

She had trouble concentrating on the payroll and ended up deducting more from her own paycheck than she'd actually earned. "At least it was my own check I messed up," she muttered, not wanting to think about what other miscalculations might have escaped her. Unwilling to risk any more errors, she put the payroll away to be finished later and seized the excuse of a sudden influx of customers to return to the sales floor.

As soon as she'd reached the showroom, however, she regretted coming out of her office. Estella Morgan was standing beside one of the display cases, drumming her manicured nails on the glass and looking daggers at the staff, each of whom was already busy with another customer.

Eve forced a smile. "Good morning, Mrs. Morgan. How can I help you?"

"I've come in to see my necklace."

She could almost hear the echo of Henry's voice. *How are you coming along with that necklace of Mrs. Morgan's?* If David was still only in the inspiration stage…

Eve braced herself. "It isn't finished, I'm afraid."

Estella Morgan was clearly in no mood to be denied. "Then I want to see the pieces. I want an idea of what it's going to look like, to make sure it's going to be appropriate for my daughter to wear."

She hadn't worried much about suitability before, Eve thought. And what was the problem, anyway? It wasn't as if this was to be a sweet sixteen gift; Estella Morgan's daughter was Eve's age.

"I'm afraid we never show unfinished jewelry, Mrs. Morgan."

"So what you're really admitting is that it isn't even started—is that it?"

Eve felt like crossing her fingers behind her back, even though she wasn't technically telling a lie. "I really don't know how far along the project is. I'm afraid David's not here just now, or you could ask him."

Estella Morgan sniffed. "I suppose that means he doesn't even have an idea."

"Inspiration may come in a flash, or only after much consideration and thinking about the best way to present a particular piece of jewelry. Either way, of course, truly wonderful design takes time to construct. Each tiny connection, each—" She felt herself fumbling for words.

She didn't have the faintest idea what David was going to do with those rings, but she suspected that whatever she said Estella Morgan would remember, and if her vague description didn't match the finished product there would be even more trouble.

Fortunately, Mrs. Morgan interrupted. "You know, I thought perhaps a new man would show some enthusiasm for the project, but instead we've just had more delays. I want you to tell Henry that I want that necklace by the end of the week. It's my daughter's birthday and I'm going to give it to her then. And he'd better make sure it's something she'll want to wear."

"I'll certainly give him your message, Mrs. Morgan."

The woman stormed out just as David and Henry came in. Mrs. Morgan stopped, blocking the doorway, and unburdened herself all over again.

When the two men broke free and came on into the showroom, Eve said pleasantly, "I guess I don't have to pass that message along after all."

"No, she made herself pretty clear," Henry agreed. He looked thoughtfully at Eve. "You know, honey, I sure like the dresses you're wearing these days. They make you look softer, somehow, than those suits you used to wear."

She called after them as they started across the sales floor toward the stairway which led to the workrooms upstairs. "May I have a minute, David?"

He said something quietly to Henry and came back toward her. "What's up, Eve?"

"I'm sorry to delay you getting to work on Mrs. Morgan's necklace, but then it's your own fault you're only now getting to work."

"I may not have been on the premises," he said mildly, "but I have certainly been working."

"Well, if your breakfasts get any longer, you'll be coming back just in time for lunch."

David dug into his pocket and pulled out a business card. "Got a pen?"

"What for? What are you doing?"

"I'm making myself a note to bring you a Danish tomorrow. Prune, maybe. Yes, I think that would be the appropriate flavor."

Eve bit her tongue as she led the way to her office.

David chose one of the overstuffed chairs beside her desk and sat down. Suddenly he bent almost double in order to inspect his toe. "Look what you did to my shoe," he said. "Stepping on my foot like that this morning when I was only—"

"That's nothing to what I'll do if you keep leading Henry on like this."

David's eyebrows climbed. "You're saying *I'm* leading him on?"

"Yes, you are. You're deliberately trying to make him believe that we...that we..."

He held up a hand. "Wait a minute here. Playing it this way was your idea in the first place."

Eve said slowly, "I suppose you have a point there. But—"

"Damn right I have a point. I distinctly remember you saying that as far as you were concerned, what Henry didn't know wouldn't hurt him."

"I only meant to let him draw his own conclusions. I certainly never intended to create some Broadway production to convince him that we're sleeping together when we're not! David," she said desperately, "it's really going to hurt him when he realizes you've only been pretending. And I don't want to hurt him."

''Well, there's a simple answer to that.'' David stood. ''Just quit pretending.''

And before she could find her voice, he'd tossed her a half-mocking salute and gone out.

CHAPTER SEVEN

IT WAS apparent to Eve from the moment the three of them walked into the conference room that the advertising agency executives were worried about losing the Birmingham on State account, and that they were deadly serious about trying to keep it. More people were already grouped around the long table than she had ever known to work on a single campaign before, leaving just three empty seats in a row along one side. And, as if that gathering wasn't convincing enough, running the entire length of the room was a row of caterer's carts lined with picture-perfect trays of ham and roast beef and turkey, vegetables and dips, fruit and cheeses and more colors and textures of bread than Eve had ever seen before.

"That's friendly of them," David murmured in her ear. "Inviting us to lunch."

"It's downright brilliant," Eve countered. "We can't walk out on a luncheon meeting without looking incredibly rude."

"Who'd want to walk out on that spread?"

"Obviously someone's already done their research on you," she said dryly. She spotted the executive who regularly handled their account—the woman was looking harried—and shook hands. Then she took one of the empty chairs, leaving the center one for Henry.

Henry, however, took the other end so that David sat in the middle. It was, Eve thought, a tactful statement of how much things had already changed at Birmingham on State. Or at least of how much Henry wanted to make it look as if things had changed.

"We've asked for this meeting," Eve began, "to discuss not only this campaign but the entire strategy of advertising Birmingham on State over the next few years."

A dark-haired woman across the table leaned forward. "That's a heavy agenda," she said with a soft, sultry laugh, "so let's start by helping ourselves to lunch. I'm Jayne Reznor, by the way." She didn't add that she was a senior partner. For Eve, at least, she didn't have to—her name was on the ad agency's letterhead. *They have brought in the heavy hitters,* she thought.

Eve was dabbing mustard on her sandwich when she heard Jayne Reznor's low voice behind her. "So you're the young man with all the new ideas," she was saying to David. "The one we have to please."

Flattery, Eve wanted to tell her, *will get you nowhere.*

"And all the questions," he agreed easily. "May I help you reach the turkey?"

Eve sat quietly through the presentation. By the time the executive who had created the questionable campaign sat down, looking even more harried, Eve had to admit that David had a point. This advertising plan was at heart no different from last year's, and the one before that. While there was nothing exactly wrong with any of them, there was nothing outstandingly right, either.

David broke the silence. "That's a competent piece of work, but we want to begin appealing to a younger market. The average age of our customers is higher than we'd like, and it's going up."

Eve wondered if he'd figured that out in little more than a week on the job, or if Henry had told him.

Jayne Reznor sat up a little straighter. "Well, David— May I call you David?"

"It's my name, Jayne," he agreed.

She dimpled just a little. "We can certainly direct the ads to a younger audience, if you like. But you must admit that the new generation doesn't generally go for the same kind of thing that your regular customer does." Her gaze rested briefly on Eve's hand, surveying the simple platinum wedding ring. "At least, *most* of the younger generation doesn't want to wear the same sort of thing their grandmothers did."

Her voice was so good-humored that for a moment Eve doubted her own ears. Had the woman really meant that insult, or had it been purely an accident of phrasing? Then Jayne's gaze flicked dismissively across the single strand of pearls at Eve's throat, and she knew there had been nothing coincidental about it.

"We can put the ads anywhere you want," Jayne went on, "but if the jewelry isn't to the taste of the people we target, we can't be blamed if they don't buy it."

"There will be some new lines," David said.

"Well, of course in that case—" The woman was eyeing him. "You know, I've just recalled a very successful campaign we did a few years ago, where we photographed the owner of the business along with women wearing his product—a different woman each month."

Henry chuckled. "As I recall, the product happened to be lingerie. I must admit I admired the idea, though I never understood how it was done. Take that shot on the ski slopes with the model in the red satin corset—"

"It was a teddy, Henry," Eve put in quietly.

"Teddy, corset, whatever. How did you keep the goose bumps from showing?"

"I have no idea. That's why we hire the best photographers." Jayne was looking warmly at David. "We could take a similar approach with jewelry. You have the sort of rugged good looks that the camera adores, David. We could make you the central theme of the ads, along with a variety of models."

Eve had heard enough to turn her off of the idea, but for Henry's sake she took a deep breath and tried to keep an open mind. Maybe there was something here worth considering, even though she hadn't happened to see it yet. "Perhaps we could partner with one of the department stores."

"What for?" Jayne asked flatly.

"To provide the clothes for the models. We could work out a cooperative advertising plan with—"

"Oh, I think we'd dispense with clothes entirely."

Eve said icily, "I beg your pardon?"

"On the models at least. You want the jewelry to get the attention, not whatever clothes the model's wearing. So if she's not wearing anything at all—"

"Nude models?"

"Oh, it would be very tastefully done," Jayne assured her. "I'm not talking about shooting centerfolds."

"Good thing, too," Henry said with a smile. "Or else the jewelry—stunning as we'd like to think it is— wouldn't get any attention at all."

"Unless we can persuade David here to create a whole new line of belly-button rings," Eve said under her breath.

David shot her a half smile as if to say he'd already thought of it.

Jayne was still inspecting David as if he were the

product for sale. "It *is* a shame you're married, but maybe we can keep that under wraps. We'll work out some ideas."

Henry said, "We'll be having an open house before long to introduce David to our clients."

"That would be the perfect kickoff for the new campaign," Jayne said promptly. "We'll have models circulating through the crowd, wearing the new jewelry."

And what else will they be wearing? Eve wondered. *G-strings and pasties?* "I hate to rain on your parade, Jayne, but our insurance company would have a collective stroke if we suggested doing anything of the kind. They'd insist we have a security guard following each model—or rather each piece of jewelry. I'm sure that's hardly the image you're thinking of."

Jayne shrugged. "I'm sure we can work it all out." She hadn't even looked at Eve. "I'll be calling you very soon, David, to bounce some new slogans around and get your feel for them."

That does it, Eve thought. "Thank you all very much for your time, but if you're going to have anything to promote, we need to get back to work designing those new lines."

On the sidewalk in front of the building, Eve was still seething. "The nerve of that woman," she muttered.

"It sounds like an interesting ad strategy to me," Henry said. "Of course we'll have to wait and see what they actually come up with. I believe I'll walk back to the store. It's such a beautiful day, and I may as well get used to having more free time." He strode off, whistling and swinging his gold-topped cane.

David hailed a cab. "That's lucky," he said as he held the door for Eve. "We need a few minutes of privacy right now."

"For what?"

"To talk about why you might want to tone down your opposition."

Eve didn't even try to hang on to her temper. "Look, David, I can see how the idea of being the centerpiece of all the ads has hit you square in the ego, but if you can't even see how that woman was manipulating you, *somebody* has to keep your feet on the ground!"

"I thought you told me just this morning that you didn't want to lead Henry on."

Eve's jaw dropped. "What on earth are you talking about? A minute ago we were discussing advertising. How did Henry get into it?"

"Because your reasons for opposing the ad campaign didn't look like sensible ones. You looked jealous."

Eve stopped breathing. There seemed to be a brick lodged in her throat. *Jealous?* He'd listened to that whole incredible conversation and the only conclusion he'd drawn from it was that she might be *jealous?*

"Face it, sweetheart," David went on easily, "if you don't want me, you really shouldn't act like a dog in the manger."

"Look here, buddy," she said furiously. "I happen to think that Jayne Reznor would flirt with the devil if she thought she could get his advertising account, but that doesn't mean I have any personal feelings about how she treats you. If you are deluded enough to believe that I was concerned about anything except Birmingham on State—"

David interrupted. "Because the truth is, if you keep acting like a green-eyed monster you can't blame Henry for getting the wrong ideas."

The store had closed for the day and the staff was gone, but Eve had hardly noticed. It had taken her most of the afternoon to straighten out the mess she'd made of the payroll and create the work schedule for the next couple of weeks, and by the time she was finished the showroom was dark except for the security lights and the glow coming down the staircase from the workrooms upstairs.

She locked her desk and climbed the stairs. Henry's workbench was littered with materials and tools, but he wasn't sitting there. Instead he was standing in the opposite corner, looking over David's shoulder. He heard Eve coming and waved her over. "Come and see what your husband's created now."

Reluctantly, she went to join them. Henry started to step aside, then took a closer look at Eve and paused. "What's wrong, dear?"

Nothing that I can talk to you about in present company, Eve thought. Though—come to think of it—why shouldn't she come straight out and tell Henry the facts, whether David was there or not? It might be better if her husband knew exactly what she had to say.

But she couldn't bring herself to do it. The sledgehammer approach might be necessary where David was concerned, but Henry deserved to be treated more gently. She'd catch him alone tomorrow and remind him, as tenderly as she could, that putting a good face on things was just part of the agreement the three of them had made, so he shouldn't jump to conclusions because of appearances.

"It's just been a long day," she said.

"Difficult customers?"

"Let's say some unusual ones. Remember that big cabochon ruby you set into a necklace right around Valentine's Day?"

Henry nodded. "Is something wrong with it?"

"The customer who ended up with it swears it came with a curse. She spent a good part of the afternoon telling me all the odd things that have been happening to her ever since her boyfriend came home with it."

David said, "A ruby with a curse? That has all kinds of possibilities. Maybe we should refund her money and turn the necklace into a tourist attraction like the Hope diamond."

"Trust me," Eve said, "the only curse attached to that ruby is the man who gave it to her." She looked at the bench and caught her breath. "Is that what you're doing with Mrs. Morgan's old rings?"

Spread across the bench was a golden net made of twisted wire and fine chain—as lacy as a dragonfly's wing, as delicate as a dream. At each spot in the scalloped pattern where wire and chain met, a random-shaped gold nugget had been mounted. Scattered over the whole were the various-size stones which had once been mounted in the rings, catching the light and sparkling like dewdrops on a spider's web.

"Who needs a ruby with a curse in order to attract tourists?" Eve said. "If Mrs. Morgan doesn't love this necklace, I'll use it to start a museum."

David said quietly, "Thank you."

He looked up at her, and Eve felt her throat tighten. It was a silly way to react, she thought. She'd given him an honest compliment, and he'd accepted it with the easy grace of a man who didn't need approval because he knew quite well that he'd produced a masterpiece. So why should she get all wobbly over a few simple words and a look?

"I do pride myself on my judgment," Henry murmured, with a fond look at David. "If you're going home now, Eve, I'll walk out with you." Assuming her answer, he went back to his bench to close and lock the roll-top cover.

Eve was still admiring the necklace. "Are you ready, David?"

He shook his head. "I'm going to stay and finish this."

"Oh." Surely it was odd that she should feel a bit disappointed at the idea of going home alone, when last night she'd have given anything to have the apartment to herself. But of course it wasn't disappointment she was feeling, she told herself, and going home alone wasn't the cause. Now she had no excuse to put off her talk with Henry till tomorrow, and that must be why she was feeling strange.

A moment later, Henry was back, hat and cane in hand.

"I'll see you later, then," Eve said.

David stood up, and almost automatically Eve offered her cheek. His lips were cool as they brushed her skin and lingered for just an instant at the corner of her mouth.

She glanced over his shoulder and caught a speculative gleam in Henry's eyes that hadn't been there just a moment ago. He looked pleased with himself.

Guilt percolated through her. Once more, with the best of intentions, she'd managed to leave her grandfather with a wrong impression.

She braced herself, and as soon as Henry had locked the door behind them she said, "Henry, I really appreciate that you haven't asked any questions about how David and I are working things out, but I really—"

"I don't need to ask," he said mildly. He stepped out

to the curb. "I wonder what the odds are on finding two cabs at this time of night."

Eve wasn't listening. "But that's the problem, you see. Just because it *looks* as if we..." She took a deep breath. "Henry, I know you hope that this marriage will produce an heir. But I have to tell you—"

He was frowning slightly. "An heir? How very Old World that sounds. Surely I didn't really say that."

Eve felt a little dizzy. Was Henry losing touch with reality, or was she? She tried to replay in her mind the various conversations they'd had, but she couldn't— there had been too many of them, over a period of months, to recall clearly who had said what. But surely... "I can't prove you actually said it in so many words, but the implication was quite clear."

He held out a hand to flag a cab. "Oh, my dear, I know better than to ask anything of the sort."

Eve opened her mouth, but no sound came out.

"And if you had stopped to think about it," he went on, "you'd have realized how foolish the whole idea would be."

"Well, yes," she managed to say. "It is, rather. That's why I—"

"Carrying the blood doesn't mean automatically having the talents and interests. Take your father, for instance. If anyone should have had diamond dust in his veins, it was him, but he couldn't have had less of an interest in anything about the business. Then there's you—"

"Henry," she protested. "You know perfectly well I love Birmingham on State!"

"Of course you do, my dear, but it's a good thing I didn't count on you taking over entirely." He smiled. "I love you, Eve, but the idea of you sitting at my workbench and trying to create a necklace gives me night-mares. Anyway, I'd be a lunatic to look that many years ahead, and more so to pin my hopes on a child who isn't even thought of yet.'' He opened the back door of the cab.

Eve sank, still speechless, onto the seat.

''Which isn't to say I wouldn't like a great-grandchild,'' Henry added thoughtfully. ''But the truth is, any offspring of yours and David's will have plenty to live up to without adding my expectations to the mix. Ah, here comes another cab. I'll see you tomorrow, my dear.''

Eve was reeling from the aftereffects of the conver-sation. Surely her conviction that he wanted an heir for the business hadn't come out of nowhere—and she was certain she hadn't made it up herself, either. Henry might not have spelled it out, but he must have said or done something that had planted the idea in her mind.

Or had she really misread her grandfather so com-pletely? Made assumptions based on what she thought Henry must want?

The cab pulled up in front of the apartment house and Eve paid the driver and walked slowly up the sidewalk, still trying to shake off her Henry-induced mental fog.

The building supervisor was coming out as she en-tered. ''I didn't know what to have them do with the boxes and stuff, Miss Birmingham,'' he said. ''Mrs. Elliot, I mean. So they just left them stacked in the el-evator lobby on your floor.''

''Boxes?'' she said vaguely.

''Yeah. I didn't like to let them go into your apartment when you weren't there. I mean, just because they said they were movers doesn't mean they're on the up-and-up. But they had to do something with the boxes.'' He was already out the front door as he finished.

Movers, she thought. She dug her mail from the small box near the entrance and rang for the elevator. It had certainly taken long enough to transport David's belongings from Atlanta to Chicago. Not that she'd exactly been looking forward to the challenge of integrating the odds and ends from his apartment into hers. She leaned against the corner of the elevator and yawned. Tomorrow would be plenty of time to worry about that.

As the elevator door opened on the eighth floor, Eve stepped out and stopped in her tracks. The lobby, normally a small but functional room, was clogged with neat stacks of cardboard boxes, plastic bins, and wooden crates, leaving only a shoulders-wide alley from the elevator to the door of her apartment.

A harsh buzz signaled that someone downstairs wanted the elevator, and Eve hastily stepped out into the narrow gap so she wasn't blocking the door.

From her new vantage point she could see that not only boxes had been deposited in the lobby. Behind one stack was a worn red-leather armchair and a matching hassock. In the farthest corner, almost completely buried, was what looked like the back of a display cabinet and a small table. She hoped the table was sturdy, because the two boxes stacked atop it were each large enough to hold a sizable television set.

A few things, she thought helplessly. *He said he'd shipped a few things!*

One whole stack of boxes displayed big red labels that said Fragile—Glass. Others were marked only with scrawled notations in black marker. One proclaimed—if she was reading it right—that it contained Kitchen Cabinets. Eve, her head reeling, found herself hoping that whoever had scribbled that note had meant the contents, not the cabinets themselves.

The elevator returned and her next-door neighbor, a bottle blonde a few years older than Eve, stepped out.

"I'm really sorry about the mess," Eve said automatically.

The woman sniffed. "I should hope so. I told the movers they couldn't leave these things here because it's a fire hazard, but they just ignored me and kept unwrapping those blankets of theirs from around the furniture."

"As soon as my husband gets home—" Eve began.

"All of this is his?" The woman's eyes took on a calculating gleam, and her tone changed almost to a purr.

Maybe she's going to offer the use of her spare bedroom, Eve thought. *Not to store all this stuff, of course, but for David to use so I'll have room for the boxes!*

Where, she wondered, were they going to put all of this? Come to that, where had David stashed it all in Atlanta? Hadn't he said he had an apartment? It must have been a large one.

She wriggled past the stack of boxes nearest the door, the ones marked Fragile. The top one rocked unsteadily, and she pulled it off the stack and carried it inside with her. She set it down on the kitchen counter and reached for the telephone.

The private number at Birmingham on State rang and rang. Had David finished and started for home? Or was he in the middle of a delicate move and just not picking up?

But finally the line clicked. "Yeah?"

"You are urgently required here," Eve said.

David didn't answer for a moment. "I was hoping you'd miss me," he said gently, "but I didn't dare think it would happen this soon."

"Give it up, David. Wishful thinking isn't going to change how I feel."

"Or—no, I've got it now. Henry laid down the law and you want to share the bad news."

"Not that, either. The movers have been here, and if you don't show up within the next half hour I will not be responsible for the contents of any box marked *Fragile.*"

"That would be my grandmother's china."

Eve was intrigued despite herself. He'd actually kept—and moved—china? She eyed the box she'd carried in. It hadn't felt heavy enough for china. Unless it was a single piece of incredible delicacy…

As if he could see her speculative look, David went on, "Feel free to open it."

"If I get an overwhelming urge to unpack, that's where I'll start. But don't count on it." She hung up the telephone and went to change her clothes for jeans and a sweater.

By the time David's key clicked in the lock, she was in the kitchen stirring a big pot of marinara sauce.

He came in carrying two more boxes and paused in the kitchen doorway. "I see what you mean. I didn't realize I had so much stuff. Or maybe it just looks like more when it's all stacked in that little space." He sniffed appreciatively. "I had no idea you were so domestic, Eve."

"I'm not, usually, but tonight I figured you'd need all the strength you could muster to shift those boxes. And besides, if I'm cooking you can't expect me to help."

"I figured there was a downside to it."

"Good luck sorting things out, by the way. You're going to need it." She waved a hand at the box she'd carried in, which stood open on the counter.

"Couldn't resist, could you?" He pulled the tissue paper that lined the box back far enough to reveal the contents.

"I only moved it because the space in the hallway was so narrow you probably couldn't have squeezed through. And since it said Fragile and you'd told me those boxes were china and invited me to take a look, I looked. You may notice," she added dryly, "that it's not china."

"It's still fragile. The movers got that much right." He picked up a scale-model plastic car—a classic red Corvette complete with decals of flames on the fenders—which had been nested carefully into the tissue paper. He sounded delighted. "I'd almost forgotten this. It's the first model kit I ever built, when I was just a little kid. It's the only one I kept."

"That's some comfort," Eve muttered. "I was afraid to open another box in case there were more."

"No more cars," he said cheerfully. "But only because I moved on fairly soon to airplanes and helicopters. I was starting to get into the knack of building model ships in bottles when I discovered it was even more fun to work with gold and diamonds." He pulled a wad of tissue from the corner of the box, unfolded it, and looked disconcerted by the dried-out half tube of glue which fell into his hand. "I didn't expect them to pack up this sort of thing, though."

"You just turned the whole project over to the movers?" Eve shook her head. "Haven't you ever moved before?" What had he said about the bridal suite? Something about it being larger than some of the apartments he'd occupied. "But you must have."

"Only short distances. I'd get a bunch of guys together and we'd have it done in an afternoon."

"And then I suppose you'd drink beer and watch sports as soon as the television was hooked up again. That explains the glue."

"What explains it? I didn't know I still had any left-over glue."

"Movers will pack anything—especially if you're paying by weight and volume. A friend of mine moved across town last year, and the crew swathed every one of her kid's broken crayons in bubble wrap."

"No wonder there are so many boxes, if they're full of this kind of thing." He put the tube of glue back in the box.

"Why didn't you put that in the garbage long ago?" Eve asked. "Of course, if you didn't empty the waste-baskets before the movers came, they'll have packed them, too—complete with junk mail and used tissues."

He looked a little woebegone, she thought. *Well, better that than amorous.*

"You can stack all the boxes in the living room in front of the bookcases," she said.

"You're sure they won't be in the way?"

"Of course they'll be in the way. They'll just be less in the way there than anywhere else I can think of. And once they're out of the hallway, you can deal with them one at a time." *And that will keep you too busy to be pushing me.* She gave the sauce another stir and put the lid on the pan.

"If that doesn't require your full attention," David began hopefully.

Eve shook her head. "I'm going to be reading the real estate ads. We start house shopping tomorrow, and with any luck we'll be moving in by Christmas. Would you like me to put on some music to get you into the spirit? Ragtime, maybe, or would you rather have a selection of Sousa marches?"

CHAPTER EIGHT

DAVID was transfixed by the stack of boxes in the lobby—he'd had no idea he had so many possessions—but that was nothing compared to the shock waiting for him in the kitchen. He had never seen Eve wearing jeans before, and he couldn't decide if she'd poured herself into this pair or simply painted them on. Either way, the effect was stunning.

He'd known from the beginning that she had a good figure—the tailored suit she'd been wearing that first day hadn't been able to conceal her proportions, no matter how hard it tried. Even if it had, the kiss at the airport would have told him she was a perfect armful. Still, the sight of her from behind in jeans...

He was still feeling a little bemused as he settled into the rhythm of shifting box after box from the lobby to the living room. Every time he walked past the kitchen door he couldn't help catching a glimpse of her. Eve stirring the pot of marinara sauce on the stove. Eve leaning on the counter with the newspaper spread out in front of her. Eve, bent over the dishwasher loading the bottom rack. That one, he decided, was his personal favorite.

He tried to focus on the boxes instead. How could he possibly still own so much stuff? He'd sold some of his furniture, but he'd sent the rest to charity before he left Atlanta—the red leather chair, display case, and table were the few exceptions. He had expected the rest of his possessions would fit in a couple of dozen boxes.

He'd been at it for an hour or so, and he'd carved a

considerable hole in the middle of the pile, when Eve brought him a tall glass of iced tea. He gratefully drank half of it at a gulp. "It's just as well I haven't bothered looking into a gym yet. By the time I shift this mountain, I figure I'll have done my weight-lifting for the next year."

"The living room's starting to look like the Great Wall of China."

"I know. As soon as I get everything inside, I'll start unpacking. If the rest of the boxes are half full of tissue paper like the first one you opened—"

"I don't think you could be that lucky." She ran a hand across the inlaid top of the table that he'd just unearthed. "This is pretty."

"I'm glad you approve of my taste."

She shot him a sideways look. "I didn't exactly say that. Take your chair, for instance. The leather's practically transparent in places, it's worn so thin."

"That was my father's favorite chair."

"I thought it must have some attraction for you beyond its native beauty," she said wryly. "Especially considering that it couldn't have had much to start with. Well, we'll just have to look for a house with a den, so you'll have a place to put it. A very intimate and preferably very dark den, so no one but you will have to look at it."

"Even a corner of the cellar will do," David said.

Eve rolled her eyes. "If you're trying to sound pitiful, you're wasting your time. You're not very good at it."

"If I'm extremely nice to you, will you make sure it's a dry corner of the cellar?"

"Knock it off, David. To tell the truth, though, I feel so sorry for you—being banished to the cellar and all—

that I'll even take a turn at carrying a box.'' She reached for the top box on a nearby stack.

He took another long drink of tea. ''I'm overwhelmed. Of course, since you were going back into the apartment anyway—'' He stopped abruptly, realizing which box she was pulling down.

Before David could warn her that it was heavier than she expected, the box caught on the corner of the one below it, and Eve gave it a tug. It came loose suddenly and plunged toward her, knocking her off balance. She fell backward.

He saw her falling as if in slow motion. She was going to land hard right on her tailbone, and the box—

It's going to crush her.

David dropped his glass, hardly hearing the crash as it shattered on the tiled floor, and dived for the box. He knew he didn't have a prayer of catching it, but perhaps he could change its path, push it aside just far enough so it didn't break a half dozen of her ribs when it hit.

He got one hand onto the end of the box and shoved as hard as he could, but his foot slipped in the spilled tea and suddenly he was flailing, too, unable to keep himself upright.

By a bare inch, the box missed Eve, hitting the hard floor with a thump which seemed to shake the building. A split second later, however, David landed on top of her. He tried to break his fall with his hands in order to save her, but a muffled whoosh warned him that he'd knocked the wind out of her anyway.

He wasn't much better off himself, and it took a minute even to figure out how he could get up without hurting her worse than he already had. Besides, they'd ended up at a very interesting angle, with his face buried exactly where the soft wool of her sweater ended and the smooth skin of her throat began. She smelled like violets—or maybe it was lilacs—mixed with a hint of oregano from the marinara sauce.

By the time he could move, Eve had gotten her voice back. "Want to tell me what you were trying to do?" she asked, sounding almost calm.

Reluctantly, he raised his head so he could look down at her. "Keep you from getting smashed."

"So instead of letting the box get me, you squashed me yourself? How thoughtful."

He stopped even thinking about getting up. "Hey, it would have been a lot worse if I'd let the saw hit you. Between that box and the tile floor, you'd have been sandwich filling."

"The what?" She turned her head to look at the box. "How do you know what's in there, anyway? It's not marked any better than the rest."

"Because I packed that one myself. It's a circular saw and all the accessories."

"A saw?" she said blankly. "You mean like to cut down trees? David, why do you own— On second thought, forget it. I don't think I want to know."

"Not a chain saw. I don't run around forests pretending to be a logger. It's the kind you'd use in a workshop to cut the shelves for a bookcase."

"Not me," she muttered. "And you packed it yourself? You let the movers take care of everything else, but you put the saw in a box?"

"Of course." He watched as she shook her head, and then he understood. "Oh, now I see what you mean. No, I didn't single it out to pack for this move. It was still boxed up from when I brought it home from my dad's house, along with the rest of his tools."

"The rest?" She sounded a little shaken. "There are more of those booby-traps?"

"They're only dangerous if you don't know what you're doing. He was a cabinetmaker, and he taught me to love tools. So I kept all of his so I could set up my own workshop one day."

"No wonder you were looking forward to a house."

He nodded. "There's also a router and a planer and a biscuit cutter and—"

"A biscuit cutter? You're positive that one doesn't belong in the kitchen?"

"No, but with all the tools there may not be room in the cellar for my den after all."

"I'll make a note to look for a very large cellar. Look, David, this isn't a particularly comfortable position. I'd kind of like to get up now, before the woman next door calls in the rescue forces."

He didn't want to get up. He wanted to kiss her till she'd forgotten how to breathe, and then take her inside the apartment, close the door, and do it again.

Her eyes narrowed. "And I'm certain you're anxious to check your saw to be sure it still works."

"Not really. If it's broken, there's nothing I can do about it." Reluctantly, however, he stood and pulled Eve to her feet.

She shifted carefully from one foot to the other, moved her head cautiously from side to side, and flexed her shoulders.

"Are you all right?" he asked quietly.

"I think so. No shooting pains anywhere, at least. It looks as if you got lucky—you won't have to explain to Henry how I happened to land in traction." She brushed off the seat of her jeans and went back into the apartment.

It was just as well she hadn't waited for an answer, David thought as he gathered up the shards of broken glass, because he wasn't sure what he'd have told her. But one thing was certain—in the era it had seemed to take that box to fall, the one thing that had never crossed his mind was how he'd explain it to Henry if Eve had been seriously injured.

He'd been far more concerned with how he would ever explain it—and come to terms with it—for himself.

They were on schedule to the minute the next morning, which Eve considered to be a small miracle in itself, considering what time it had been when David had wearily hoisted the last box onto the barricade that now concealed the bookcases along one end of the living room.

"Though the way our luck's been running," Eve muttered as she took her last sip of coffee and set her cup on the hall table, "the cab will have a flat tire, or a building will collapse into the street in front of us, or there'll be an accident on Lake Shore Drive—"

David wriggled the door handle. "Or the lock will jam."

"That's a good one."

"I'm serious." He demonstrated. The dead bolt had receded when he turned the catch, but now it was stuck and no matter how he fiddled, it would not work properly. "It's loose inside, so the door won't lock—or if it does, it may not open again."

"Oh, that's a cheerful thought," Eve muttered. "I'll call the super. And if his wife tells me he's just left for Antarctica or somewhere else that's almost as handy, I won't be responsible for what I do."

David said absently, "See if you can find me a screwdriver."

"There's no point in looking, because I don't own one."

He looked over his shoulder. "Don't you ever want to tighten a drawer knob?"

"That's what building superintendents are for, so don't raise those arrogant eyebrows at me."

"Everybody should be able to— Never mind. There's a box of hand tools somewhere in my stuff."

"*Somewhere?* Oh, that's helpful. Any idea which level it's in, or should I just square off the whole area and start an archeological dig?"

"I keep telling you, if you'd just have breakfast you'd feel better in the mornings," he muttered and went to look for the toolbox.

Eve tried the lock herself, but she had to admit it was every bit as balky as David had said it was. Once she even managed to get the dead bolt extended, though she didn't quite know how she'd done it. But of course with the bolt sticking out, the door wouldn't close at all.

When David came back with a big gray plastic case, Eve eagerly moved back from the door and said, "Of course, this makes the search for a house easier."

"Why? Because you won't feel so sad about leaving here?"

"No. Because now that I know you're a handyman, I can look for a fixer-upper."

He gave her an abstracted smile and went to work on the lock. A few minutes later it was working smoothly again, but the delay meant that they were late to work for the third day in a row.

"I should have known better than to call off the pool," Henry said mildly when they came in, "no matter what you said, Eve."

She told him about the lock. His eyes began to twinkle, and Eve braced herself.

"Though maybe we should just form a new one," Henry murmured, "with the daily winner being whoever comes closest to guessing the reason you'll give for being late." He looked past her to David. "I was cleaning off my workbench this morning and found a stone I'd forgotten all about—an unusually nice sapphire, five or six carats. I bought it—oh, it must have been a couple of years ago. Thought maybe you'd like to have a look at it."

Eve wasn't a bit surprised that Henry could mislay a five-carat sapphire for a year or two and not give it a thought, but she was glad there weren't any customers within earshot to be shocked by the idea. "Before you two go off to play," she said, "I need to ask. David, did you finish Mrs. Morgan's necklace before you came home last night?"

Behind her, one of the sales staff, who was just hanging up the telephone, stifled a giggle. It didn't take a genius to figure out what she was thinking, Eve decided. *The newlyweds must have had too many other things to do to talk about work.* The only dignified thing to do, she told herself, was to ignore it.

David nodded. "I want to look it over again, just to be sure I didn't miss anything—but that won't take long."

"Then I'll call to tell her she can pick it up later today."

Someone—one of the staff, no doubt—had left a folded newspaper lying on her desk, open to the society section. Eve glanced at it as she waited for Estella Morgan to answer the telephone. The story about her wedding ran across the top half of the page. She left a message for Mrs. Morgan and settled down to read.

The way the reporter gushed over the ceremony, the wedding dinner, and the guest list made it sound like the most romantic marriage in a century. Eve finished reading and pushed the newspaper aside. There was an uncomfortable feeling in the pit of her stomach. She couldn't quite decide whether she was feeling cynical about how simple it had been to fool people or still uneasy because the idea of putting on a show went so much against the grain.

A little of each, perhaps, she concluded. She put the newspaper safely in the bottom drawer and went out to the sales floor to track down and thank whichever member of the staff had brought it for her.

It was an unusually quiet morning for Birmingham on State, and at the moment there were no customers in the showroom at all. But Eve was pleased to see that the two staff members weren't simply standing there with nothing to do. One was cleaning the glass display case closest to the front door, wiping off the ever-present fingerprints, while the other straightened rings in another of the cases, tilting each one so the stone caught the spotlight shining down on it. They were talking as they worked.

Eve was halfway across the showroom when she caught a name and realized what—or rather, who—the two salespeople were discussing. "I never thought of Travis Tate as a family man," one said.

"Neither did I. But he sure is one now."

Eve's nerves tingled. Travis Tate as a family man... well, she hadn't thought of him that way herself, either—at least at first. "What's happened with Travis?"

she asked, keeping her voice carefully casual. "He was just here on Monday."

"I know," said one of the clerks. "I'm the one who talked to his secretary that morning when she called. That's why he was back in your office when you came in—he said you wouldn't mind if he used your phone, and he just walked in."

Eve frowned. "She called here? Why didn't she use his cell phone?"

The clerk shrugged. "She said she'd tried it. It wasn't working, or something, so she was calling every store in the Loop, trying to catch him. She didn't say what it was about, but she was certainly relieved when I told her he was here."

Eve felt a bit foolish. She was being far too sensitive to nuances—hearing Travis's name and instantly assuming that something earthshaking must had happened to him. "Probably just a customer he needed to see in a hurry."

"That's what I thought," the clerk said, "though she sounded more rattled than I've ever heard her. Anyway, that's all I knew till this morning when she called back to thank me for finding him and told me that she'd been trying to run him down that morning because his wife had gone into labor."

"With twins," the other clerk said with relish.

Eve felt as if the ground had fallen out from under her, leaving her weightless and adrift.

I told him to go home and make his marriage work, she thought wryly. *I just didn't expect that he'd be quite so enthusiastic about the effort.*

"The babies were early, of course," said one of the clerks. "I suppose that's why he was out here instead of at home—because they weren't expected for another month or so. Anyway, that's the story. Twin boys. He'll probably be passing out pictures his next trip.''

I doubt it, Eve thought absently. *Unless it makes a difference that they're boys—because he never said a word about having two little girls.*

Instinctively, she turned toward her office again. She wanted to be alone. She was having trouble getting a deep breath, and in fact, she felt as if she might faint— even though at the same time every one of her senses seemed keener than ever before. The spotlights were suddenly so bright that they hurt her eyes, and the scent of air freshener threatened to choke her like a toxic cloud. The soft murmur of the sound system seemed to pound against her eardrums as she crossed the room, and in a sudden blessed silence between numbers, she heard one of the clerks murmur, ''Did I say something wrong? Maybe I shouldn't have told her. You don't suppose she really did have a thing for him, do you?''

The other one said, ''Are you kidding? A woman who has David Elliot wouldn't think twice about a jerk like Travis Tate.''

From the corner of her eye, she saw the first clerk nod wisely.

A jerk like Travis...

They were wrong, of course. They didn't know the whole story, so they couldn't possibly understand.

But her mental protest felt weak and feeble. The indignation she had expected to feel at the clerks' assessment of Travis didn't materialize. It wasn't only the clerks who saw him that way, she reminded herself. David had thought the same thing, though he'd only met the man once. What was it he'd said? Something about how Travis had miscalculated...

David had made it sound as if Travis had led her on

deliberately. As if their falling in love hadn't been an accident that was beyond their control. As if Travis had actually lied about being separated from his wife…

The floor seemed to rock under her as realization hit. *But it was a lie,* she thought. *It has to have been a lie.*

She could check it out on the calendar, of course— but she didn't need to. She didn't have to count the months to know that Travis had been earnestly telling her about his failed marriage at right about the same time that his wife had become pregnant.

Fury licked along every nerve in her body. While Eve had been torturing herself with her decision, Travis had been enjoying all the comforts of home. While she had been contemplating the painful truth that she must sacrifice her own happiness for the sake of his children, he had been thinking only of his own desires. And by the time Eve had reached her heart-wrenching choice, Travis had quite possibly already known that his wife was expecting again.

He'd certainly known it last week at the airport, when he'd told her how hard he'd tried to resurrect his marriage and how hopeless the effort was…

But she wasn't simply livid at Travis, she realized. She was angry with him for the lies he had told, yes— but she was also angry with herself for being so naive. She had trusted him—and she had almost fallen for the biggest lie of all. *Had* fallen, in fact—for she had never once questioned the essential truth of what he'd told her. If it hadn't been for Travis's two small daughters and her own conscience, which had so stubbornly refused to hurt a pair of innocent children, she might have plunged straight on, still believing him—and she'd be caught in the middle of this mess right now.

What a fool she had been.

The misunderstood husband with the cold and unloving wife must be the oldest story in the human repertoire. No doubt it was still around because it worked so well—and as long as gullible women like her listened in sympathy, it would continue to be the favorite line of wandering husbands.

Idiot, she told herself. *You wanted so desperately to believe that you made it easy for him.* She wondered if Travis had been cynically laughing at her the whole time. The idea made her feel a little sick. Or had he managed to delude himself, too? Had he, in his own feeble way, loved her? Or had he only wanted to use her?

Had he ever intended to leave his wife at all? *Only after he was certain of you,* rumbled a voice in the back of her brain. She thought it sounded uncomfortably like David murmuring in her ear, because hadn't he said very much the same thing? *And only because you're Henry's heir,* the voice went on relentlessly, *so he figured the payoff would be worth all the fallout.*

No wonder Travis had been so rude to David that morning, she thought. He'd made those nasty comments about David having married her to get his hands on the business, about him suddenly having a lot to lose, because Travis had expected to be standing in those shoes himself. He'd almost been talking about himself.

Eve only half heard the tiny chime which noted the entrance of a customer, but there was no mistaking the strident note in Estella Morgan's voice as she bore down on one of the salesclerks. "This is a very inconvenient time for me to have to come all the way downtown," she said. "Especially after having been here just yesterday. Of course, heaven knows how long this project would have taken if I hadn't come in to make a fuss about it.''

''Mama,'' a small voice protested. ''It's not the clerk's fault.''

Eve took a deep breath, shoved Travis to the far reaches of her brain, pasted a smile on her lips, and walked across the sales floor to where Estella Morgan and her small, dark-haired daughter were face-to-face with a clerk.

The clerk looked terrified. ''I'll help Mrs. Morgan,'' Eve murmured to her. ''Would you ask Mr. Elliot to come down, and tell him Mrs. Morgan is here?'' The clerk squeaked in relief and vanished up the stairs.

Estella fixed Eve with a beady stare. ''So where is it? You said my necklace was finished.'' Her gaze swept around the showroom. ''I don't see it anywhere.''

Eve kept her voice low and pleasant. ''That's because we don't display custom jewelry before the owner has approved it. It would be very rude of us to let someone else see your necklace before you did. If you'll come with me—'' She led the two women across the sales floor to the small consultation room and smiled at Estella's daughter. ''I think you'll be very pleased.''

The young woman looked less than convinced. ''This whole thing is pretty ridiculous,'' she grumbled. ''No matter what you do with it, it's still just junky old jewelry. Anyway, it wasn't *my* idea to do this. I'd have thrown all that old stuff away and bought something really nice.''

Estella's voice suddenly took on a purr. ''But, Jess, darling, Eve assures me that the junky old jewelry you object to has become, under the master's touch, an heirloom.''

Eve's head was beginning to throb a little. *If Mrs.*

Morgan doesn't love this, she had told David last night, *I'll use it to start a museum.* If it wasn't possible to please the woman, she might just follow through. It would serve Estella Morgan right.

David appeared, carrying a rolled-up black velvet cloth. Behind him, beaming, was Henry. ''I don't mean to barge in,'' he said, shaking Estella's hand, ''but I just had to see what you think of this.''

David came around the table to stand beside Eve, who started to get up. He laid a hand on her shoulder, urging her back into her chair, and with the snap of his wrist unrolled the velvet atop the table.

One instant there was nothing to look at except the light-absorbing velvet, as black as a cave. The next, almost magically, the golden net had appeared, twinkling under the lights. If he'd rehearsed it, Eve thought, he couldn't have created a more theatrical, more impressive display.

There was a long silence inside the consultation room.

Generally, Eve knew, that was a good indicator—the sign of a customer who had been knocked sideways by the beauty she was seeing. With Estella Morgan, however, all bets were off.

Fifteen seconds ticked by before Jess put out a tentative finger, touching the necklace as if she expected it to dissolve under even the lightest touch. Eve tried to smother her sigh of relief.

Jess looked from the necklace to David. ''You're incredible.'' She sounded as if she was a long distance away.

That's enough, Eve thought idly. *Let's not encourage the man to be more arrogant than he already is.*

''Wait till my friends see this. They'll all want you to make something for them.''

Maybe it won't take belly-button rings to attract the younger crowd after all.

"But I'm ahead of them all, because I own the very first thing you've made since you got here," Jess said. She sounded very young, and very proud.

Not quite, Eve thought. *My wedding ring was first.*

David was smiling at the young woman. "I hope you'll always enjoy it as you do today."

Eve was momentarily taken aback, until she stopped to think. Of course he hadn't wanted to diminish the young woman's joy by pointing out that she was wrong—not when it was something so unimportant, at any rate. That should have been obvious to Eve herself, with her years of experience in customer service. What was the matter with her?

Estella Morgan cleared her throat. "It's not quite what I expected," she said flatly.

A silence descended over the little room. Eve could hear her own heartbeat. "Well, that's the point, isn't it?" she said pleasantly. "We specialize in the unique—that's why you brought your rings to Birmingham on State in the first place. If you want something ordinary, there are a hundred places to get it."

"Oh, Mother," Jess said impatiently. "Don't be a fool. Can't you see how wonderful he is?"

He, Eve noted. Not *it.* The creator, not the work. She looked closer, and saw that there was outright adoration in the girl's eyes as she looked at David. "Will you help me put it on?"

He smiled at Eve. "Your department, I believe."

Feeling awkward, she fastened the golden net around Jess Morgan's throat, where it lay perfectly.

Estella Morgan gathered her handbag and stood up.

"It looks like a dog collar," she said tightly. "But I suppose if it satisfies you, Jess, that's all that counts."

Henry walked the Morgans to the door. Eve hoped he was planning to extract a check from Estella before she got away.

As soon as Eve was certain they were out of range, she sagged in her chair. "That could have been a close one," she said. "What did she think you were going to do with those rings? Saw them all apart and then just hook them back together like the links of an old chain?"

David looked at her intently.

Somewhere deep inside Eve, a bubble of warmth began to form and grow, and ever so slowly the heat began to spread out until her entire body was immersed in it. And suddenly she realized what was happening to her. What had been happening for days.

When the clerk had told her about Travis's wife, Eve had been furious at his betrayal. But what she hadn't realized until just this instant was that she had not been hurt by the revelation.

Sometime in the last few months—maybe just in the last few weeks—the wounds he had left on her had healed, until now Travis didn't have the power to hurt her anymore. But it was only when she was put to the test that she'd realized it.

She didn't understand how it had happened, and she knew that total comprehension might be a long time coming. But that didn't matter right now. She was incredibly lucky not only to be over him but to finally know that she was free. She took a deep breath of relief, and felt that she could float right off the floor with happiness.

I must have already known what he was. Without even realizing it, I was healing.

But something about that picture didn't feel right. It didn't seem real.

Confused, she looked up at David, and abruptly, as though she were looking through a microscope that had suddenly come into focus, she saw the truth.

She wasn't free. She was far from being free.

But it wasn't because she was still wrapped up in Travis. It was because of David. She had thought she was still in love with Travis, when the truth was that she had never loved him. Had never even known what love was…until now. That was what was wrong with her. Somewhere in the last few days she had done the unthinkable.

She had fallen in love with her husband.

CHAPTER NINE

SHE had convinced herself that because of Travis she would never be able to love again, and so she had thought that no matter what she did, she was invulnerable.

As if, she thought, Travis had been some sort of disease and exposure to him had given her immunity to ever catching the bug again. Well, he'd been a disease, all right—no question about that. But he hadn't left her with any resistance, for what she had thought was love for Travis had instead been only infatuation. And so when she'd blithely exposed herself to the real thing, thinking she was safe, she'd come down with a raging case.

She'd fallen in love with David.

Looking back, she could see quite easily how it had happened. With any other man, under any other set of circumstances, she would have continued to keep her guard up. But she hadn't thought it necessary with David, because they'd both been so open about their intentions and their feelings. He was, she thought, so very dependable....

In fact, she realized now that it was too late, that very solidity of his was part of what made him so dangerous. Because it was safe to rely on him, she had let herself trust. She had let herself grow to like him. And then she had crossed the line—so now she would have to pay the price.

"Eve?" David said. "Are you all right?"

She tensed, terrified that he would be able to read her thoughts. "Fine," she said, and knew that her voice was unusually high and thin. She groped for some explanation and hit on one that had the advantage of being true—as far as it went. "My shoulder hurts. I think maybe I pulled something last night when I fell."

He moved around behind her chair. "Show me where."

She shook her head. "It's nothing, really. I'm stiff, that's all."

His fingertips came to rest on the tops of her shoulders, gently probing to find the sore spots.

Eve's muscles tingled with the contact. She wanted to jump up, to break the connection and escape the electrical current that his touch seemed to be sending through her. At the same time, she wanted to sit absolutely still, leaning closer to him and losing herself in the comfort of his touch.

David's hands stilled, his palms cupped around the base of her neck. "Everything feels all right. But maybe you should go home and put some heat on it."

The only kind of heat I want, she thought, *is from your hands.* "No," she said, too quickly. "I have too much to do to take the day off."

From the door of the little room, one of the clerks spoke. "Ms. Reznor from the ad agency is on the phone."

"I'll take it in my office," Eve said. David didn't try to stop her from standing up. But had he released her reluctantly, or had that been just her imagination? Was she seeing what she wanted to see?

The clerk looked hesitant. "She asked for David."

"Of course," Eve said, trying to keep her voice light. "How silly of me."

''There's a speaker phone in your office, isn't there?''
David asked. ''We can both talk to her.''

''Oh, I'm sure it's not my reaction Jayne wants.''
David frowned a little, and Eve pulled herself up short.
''Goodness,'' she said sweetly. ''Am I sounding like a
green-eyed monster again? Poor Jayne, she does bring
out the worst in me.''

And that was one of the most truthful things she'd
ever said, Eve admitted as she escaped to her office.
Except that it wasn't necessarily Jayne Reznor who had
prompted Eve's attitude. Yes, she'd felt like going up in
smoke during that meeting with the ad agency when
Jayne had flirted with David right under Eve's nose. *Too
bad you're married,* indeed... But she'd reacted almost
the same way a few minutes ago when Jess Morgan had
looked at David with adoration in her eyes.

Worse, she'd not only been jealous, she'd been too
short-sighted to see what was happening to her. For days
she'd been walking along the edge of a cliff blindfolded,
without enough sense to stop in her tracks until she
could figure out where she was and how to get back to
safety. Instead she'd gone right ahead and plunged off
the edge.

That odd feeling she'd had while reading the story
about their wedding—now she knew that it hadn't been
cynicism she'd felt, nor uneasiness. It had been regret
that it wasn't all real, that her marriage wasn't the romantic dream the reporter had pictured.

And now she understood why she'd reacted so oddly
when David had suggested that they revise the rules. Eve
had been irritated and annoyed at him for trying to
change the terms of their agreement after the fact. But
what she hadn't wanted to admit, even to herself, was
that she'd also been intrigued. Tantalized. Tempted.

And—though she hadn't admitted it even to herself—pleased that she had the power to lure him. Gratified that he wanted her.

Because she certainly wanted him.

But what on earth was she going to do about it? It was easy enough to ask the question, but the answer was far from simple.

David had suggested that they make their marriage a real one, in much the same way that Henry had done all those years ago with the wife his family had found for him. Yesterday, David's suggestion had seemed to Eve like far too much—too much intimacy, too much involvement, too much investment in one another. Today, it seemed to be not nearly enough.

But was she being too idealistic? Was she asking too much? Could she settle for what he was offering?

Together Henry and Sarah had found companionship and common interests. They had built a family together. And in the end, they had shared a kind of love—though even Henry had admitted it had been a long way from the dizzying, breath-taking kind. *Head over heels doesn't last,* Henry had told her. *Dependable does.*

There was not a doubt in her mind that what David offered would be steady, reliable…dependable. But was dependable enough, when it was head over heels that she wanted?

Wrong question, Eve, she told herself. What she wanted was one thing, but what she could actually have was something else altogether. It wasn't a matter of getting what she wanted, because that was out of her reach.

The choice was whether to seize what she could have and be satisfied with it, or to have nothing at all.

Eve was on the sales floor late that afternoon when a young couple came in. She recognized them immediately, both from the store and from the visit she and David had made to the gem room at the natural history museum, the day after their wedding.

Our honeymoon trip, she thought.

Today the pair had an air of determination about them that told her there was no need for a sales pitch, because their decision had been made before they came through the door. She greeted them warmly and took them straight to the small consultation room.

Just going back into the room made her feel a little breathless, as if the sudden, stunning rush of feelings she had experienced that morning was still there, hovering ghostlike over the small table.

She showed them a half dozen diamond rings, and she knew the instant they saw the right one. She watched as the young man slipped the ring onto his fiancée's finger, and saw the softness in the young woman's face as she looked at her new ring and then up at him. Eve felt as if she should excuse herself, because it was the most private of moments.

The quiet happiness in the two faces should have been enough to confirm for her that she'd made the right decision when she'd told David she didn't want an engagement ring. It would have been hypocritical to wear one when the feeling between them was nothing like this young couple's love.

But now it was a little more complicated than that. Now she found herself wishing that she hadn't been quite such a stickler on the question of diamonds. She had her wedding ring, of course—but it didn't make quite the same lavish statement as a diamond would have. If she was wearing his diamond, she could at least pretend that it was a symbol of love. She could pretend that he truly cared for her.

And that would be just like pretending the lake is dry, she told herself. *Because pretending doesn't make it so.*

David turned his key in the lock and said, "That's a comfort. It actually works."

It took Eve a moment to remember what he was talking about, because so much had happened since the lock had failed that morning. "You had doubts? It's your turn to cook, by the way."

He gave her a sideways look. "Sure you want to risk it? For all you know, my skills in the kitchen don't go beyond fixing a bologna sandwich and phoning for pizza."

"I don't think we have bologna," she said. "So I guess that leaves pizza."

"I might be able to manage something else." He inspected the contents of the refrigerator. "Maybe if I ply you with a glass or two of wine, you won't notice if I burn the main course."

"Sounds like a great idea. I forgot to ask you what Jayne Reznor had to say." Eve was proud of herself for managing to sound almost casual.

"More of the same." He handed her a glass.

"How great you'd look on a sailboat with a model wearing nothing but sapphires the color of the water?" *He would, too,* Eve thought. *That's part of the problem.*

"That's about the size of it. I told her if she could figure out a way to get around your allergy to the sun so you could be the model, we'd give it some thought."

"You did *what?*"

"Not really. I told her that for somebody who desperately wants to keep an account, she sure has a funny way of going about it."

Delight bubbled up inside Eve. "I should have known you had more sense than to fall for her line."

"Of course," David said thoughtfully, "we could restrict everything to indoor settings where you wouldn't be exposed to the sun—"

"Too public for me."

"I agree, but since I'm not getting anywhere in private I thought it was worth a try."

You're getting farther than you think. Eve was a little afraid to stay around for fear of what she might say, so she took her wineglass with her while she changed clothes. When she came back the sounds of pans banging and the occasional swearword discouraged her from even looking into the kitchen.

But the living room was no more inviting. It would have been uncomfortable enough with the wall of boxes in place, but David had been in a hurry to find his toolbox this morning, so he'd dug through the stack and left an untidy heap that almost blocked the doorway. Eve sighed, set down her glass, and started to sort out the mess. This time she was wise enough to test the weight of each box before trying to lift it.

"Somehow the division of labor tonight isn't quite what I expected it to be," she muttered. "Maybe I shouldn't have been so eager to avoid the kitchen."

She lifted a carton marked Fragile and put it on top of a pile. The one underneath was a box she'd seen before—it was the one that had caught her eye last night in the elevator lobby because it was labeled Kitchen Cabinets. This time curiosity got the better of her. Reaching for the box cutter that David had left lying atop the empty carton that had held his tools, she slit the packing tape.

Her suspicion had been correct—the movers had simply emptied the shelves and drawers in David's kitchen and dumped everything into a box, with no regard as to whether it was worth shipping halfway across the country. There was an opened box of dehydrated potatoes, a can of chicken noodle soup, a discolored rubber spatula, the lid to a long-gone jar, a battered skillet, two packages of microwave popcorn, a paring knife with an age-blackened wooden handle, and a plastic box with a melted corner. Here and there among the food and utensils were bits of paper—a grocery list so old it was yellowed along the edges, a phone number scrawled on a paper towel, what looked like a design for a ring sketched on the torn corner of an envelope, an advertisement ripped from a magazine—that seemed to have fallen from between the pages of a week-by-week calendar. Down in a corner of the box she spotted a can opener and a corkscrew. No doubt, she deduced, those were the two things no self-respecting bachelor could do without.

Eve looked at the assortment for a long moment, feeling just a little faint and hoping that there wasn't a box somewhere containing things the movers had taken out of his refrigerator.

"I can't believe I just turned this man loose in my kitchen," she muttered. "What have I done?"

Whatever else happens, she thought, *life won't ever be dull as long as David's around.*

She took a long, deep breath and tried to assess the feeling that was spreading through her. It wasn't joy exactly, she thought. It wasn't quite happiness, either.

Finally she recognized it. She was feeling secure, contented, at peace.

What she was experiencing was a far cry from the crazy, head-over-heels excitement that most people associated with being in love. But that didn't make the feeling less real, or less dynamic, or less important. Now she knew what Henry had meant. *Head over heels doesn't last,* he'd said. *Dependable does—and it's a lot more comfortable, too.*

More comfortable—but in its own way, no less enjoyable.

She piled as much of the mess as she could into the skillet and carried it all into the kitchen. She could sort some of it out while he finished cooking.

Though she wouldn't have been surprised to encounter black clouds of smoke, the mixture sizzling on the stove smelled delicious. She thought she detected dill, and lemon, and the rich scent of fresh salmon.

David stopped stirring and looked up. He'd shed his jacket, his tie was draped over the back of one of the high stools at the counter, and the collar of his white shirt was open. His own wineglass stood beside the skillet. "Oh, good, you've been unpacking. Did you happen to find my favorite knife?"

"I presume it's your favorite because it's the only one you own?" Eve pulled it out from under the box of instant potatoes. "This thing looks as if it's been on a perpetual camping trip."

"It's had its share of travel. Careful, it's sharp." He reached for the knife just as Eve held it out. His hand bumped hers, and the handle seemed to leap out of her fingers. It spun almost lazily in the air and fell, the blade brushing against the side of her wrist as she tried to draw back.

David was right—it was sharp. So sharp, in fact, that at first she didn't even feel it slice. Only when she saw the blood seeping from the hairline cut did she realize she'd been hit.

David grabbed for a towel.

Eve tried to fend him off. "It's only a scratch."

"It still needs to be cleaned."

"Considering everything that was in that box," she said wryly, "perhaps you're right. But don't get blood on the towel, it's too hard to get it out." She let him hold her wrist under cold water, and told him where to find disinfectant and bandages.

When David returned, she was absentmindedly stirring the contents of the skillet and looking at a sketch drawn on the back of a paper napkin which was lying on the counter next to the stove. "What's this?"

He looked a little sheepish. "I was trying out your idea."

"*My* idea?"

"Yes. For the rings. This morning you said I could have just taken the Morgan woman's rings, cut them apart, strung them together like the links of a chain, and made a bracelet."

"David, I was kidding. It was the most outlandish thing I could think of, on the spur of the moment."

"I know. But it's still not a bad idea. Are you sure you don't want to go into design?"

She looked again at the drawing. He'd obviously done the sketch very quickly, but the structure was there nonetheless. It was a chunky sort of bracelet, not quite massive but nothing like the delicate art of Jess Morgan's necklace. But for the right sort of occasion, to set off the right sort of clothes… "It's just a little strange. Kind of… I don't know. Off kilter."

"It has its own sort of style," he said stubbornly. "Not for the average woman, perhaps, but it would be eye-catching."

"And for those younger clients you're trying to woo, that sort of thing might be just the ticket."

He nodded. "Jewelry that makes you look twice, but not just because it's pretty."

"Well, hang on to the drawings. The next time a client comes in with a handful of rings she wants re-engineered…"

"I was thinking of looking through old stock to re-cycle. Every jewelry store has a few things lying around that are never going to sell in their present form."

"Try the very back of the main safe," Eve said. "That's where our mistakes tend to migrate. I'll look tomorrow if you like."

David poured disinfectant over her cut and covered it with a bandage that ran across her wrist and down onto her hand. "We make a pretty good team, you know."

Eve studied his handiwork. "Gee, I'm sorry," she said lightly. "But this member of the team can't take her turn cleaning up the kitchen tonight."

"That wasn't what I meant, Eve." He turned back to the sizzling skillet.

A pretty good team…

And, she told herself firmly, there was nothing so wrong with that.

She'd like to have more, of course. What she wanted was a union of soul mates. But if she couldn't have that—and she wasn't such a fool as to think she could snap her fingers and make David fall for her as she'd fallen for him—then the idea of being *a pretty good team* wasn't so bad at all. A team at work, a team at home, a team at play….

There really was only one answer. If her choices were to have half a loaf or to have nothing at all, then she'd take the bit of bread she could have and be satisfied with it.

In any case, she told herself, she wasn't lowering her standards—she was raising them. She had settled for a marriage built on the foundation of respect and loyalty, because she had believed she couldn't have love. Now, however…

It would be a one-sided sort of love, that was true. Since it hadn't entered into the original terms, it wouldn't be fair even to hope that David would ever feel it. But that didn't—couldn't—keep her from loving him, and from acting on that love.

He had predicted that she would want and need physical intimacy. And he'd been both right and wrong, for she did indeed want intimacy. But only with him.

David looked over his shoulder. "If you're not too wounded to get a couple of plates—"

Something in the way she was looking at him seemed to stop him cold.

She found herself moving toward him as though he were a magnet and she was steel—except that she felt neither cold nor rigid. She let her fingertips rest against the starched white front of his shirt. Just ten small spots of contact, she thought. Only a few square inches. And yet she felt as connected to him as if they were bound together.

She looked up and said, "Kiss me."

"Is there an audience here that I'm unaware of?"

Eve shook her head. "Just kiss me." Her hands drifted upward and locked together at the back of his neck.

Suddenly he sounded as if he was having trouble getting his breath. "Eve, what hit you all of a sudden?"

"You did," she whispered, and tugged. "You said whenever I decided to change the rules, to let you know. I'm changing them, David."

She'd been preoccupied every other time when he'd kissed her—by Travis in the airport, by the crowd at their wedding, by the shock of his suggestion that she sleep with him. Even so, it had been abundantly clear to her that David was no amateur. Despite the handicap of an audience, he had come close to turning her the consistency of chocolate syrup, melting her knees and making her forget everything around her. Now Eve relaxed and gave herself up completely to the adventure of discovering how it felt to kiss him with no restrictions and no reservations.

It felt wonderful. There was no other word, she mused, though without a doubt if she could concentrate for a minute or two, she would come up with a better one. But she couldn't concentrate. She didn't even want to try. Her mind had narrowed until the only thing left in it was David and the sensations he was rousing. Her vision was blurry, her ears were buzzing. Only her senses of taste and touch seemed to be working, and they'd kicked into overdrive.

When David raised his head, he was breathless. "Dammit, Eve, why do I suddenly get the feeling that you just handed me an apple?"

She said vaguely, "Apple?"

"And it feels like there's a snake wrapped around my ankles, too."

"Oh," she said. "Are you off balance because I'm tempting you? Good. Because that's exactly what I intended to do.'' She smiled up at him. ''Don't forget to turn off the stove, David. Because dinner will wait.''

David had figured out long ago that she was at her most dangerous when she was smiling. But the simple knowledge wasn't enough to protect him. That particular smile of hers was enticing enough to make a robot lose its head. How could any mere male be expected to stand up against it, especially when it was combined with a warm and clinging body, soft and promising kisses, and an invitation he had dreamed of?

Though why he was even considering standing up against it was beyond David's comprehension.

Because she changed her mind too suddenly, he thought. Just yesterday she'd accused him of falling in lust and said she had no intention of modifying the rules. Now she was actively seducing him. But why?

By reminding her of what she was missing, he'd obviously succeeded in reawakening her physical desires.

Or had he? What had Henry said to her last night? She hadn't told him. *And I didn't ask,* David recalled. Of course, they'd both had their minds on other things— namely the stack of boxes in the elevator lobby. Or had she been preoccupied by something else, as well? Something Henry had said?

Surely not, David thought. He suspected Henry Birmingham knew exactly what he was doing, and surely the old man realized there would be no advantage in playing the heavy at this late date.

Which brought him to a far more realistic concern. Eve, he was convinced, still believed that Travis Tate was the only man she could ever care for. But what about David? Did she regard him as only a handy substitute to slake her physical desires? When she took him to her bed, would she be pretending he was Travis?

He looked down at her left hand, spread across his chest as if she was trying to put her brand on him. His ring gleamed on her finger.

She can try to pretend, he thought, almost grimly. *But she isn't going to succeed.*

He reached past her and turned off the heat under the skillet.

His Eve hadn't just handed him an apple, she'd presented him with the whole pie. And he intended to enjoy every last bite.

Eve was impatient with him, and even just a little afraid. Why was he resisting? Making love had been his idea in the first place. What could have changed his mind since yesterday?

But before she could attempt to figure it out, he had obviously made his decision—just as she had made hers—and suddenly all the initiative she'd possessed was snatched out of her hands so suddenly that it left her breathless.

He picked her up and carried her down the hall. "Not that I have anything against making love in kitchens," he said as he pushed open her bedroom door with his shoulder. "But we're going to take our time."

"Good," Eve was starting to say when he kissed her, and this kiss was so much more demanding, so explosive, that for a very long time she couldn't say anything at all. But there was no need for words, when their bodies said it all so much more clearly anyway.

She hadn't had time to wonder what making love with him would be like, and it was just as well—for no amount of imagination could have met the reality. First he made her ache with desire, and then with satisfaction—until ultimately, sated and drowsy with contentment, she lay in his arms, her mind drifting. How could she ever have doubted how she felt about him? It should have been obvious. This was so right...

"Henry will be happy," she murmured.

David raised his head a half inch, as if anything more would require too much effort. "You're thinking about Henry?"

"Not really." She yawned. "I was mostly thinking about you."

"That's better."

She let herself float away again. "Now you have everything you want," she murmured, and almost before she'd finished the sentence she was asleep.

Eve was awake not long after dawn, lying very still and watching David sleep. Those expressive eyebrows of his were drawn together this morning as if he was frowning, or maybe concentrating. Trying to wring the maximum from the last few minutes of sleep perhaps. Her heart felt soft and almost too large for her chest.

How very different this was from the first morning they'd awakened together, she thought. That time, all she'd been able to think of was how quickly she could escape the situation. Today she wanted to tease him awake and then snuggle down into his arms to spend the whole day making love.

But another part of her felt too self-conscious to do anything of the kind. Last night had been incredible, magical—but this morning the cool light of reason had returned. Last night she had felt like a temptress, and she'd acted on the impulse. This morning the more logical half of her brain was in charge, reminding her that she couldn't just forget about work because it was a bit inconvenient.

More importantly, however, it reminded her that she couldn't forget about their agreement just because it, too, had suddenly become a bit of an inconvenience to her. Because the arrangement stood—despite her change of heart, they still had an agreement to create a simple, stable marriage without emotional entanglements.

For her, last night had altered everything. Making love with him had been, for her, an even more meaningful vow than the promise she'd made at their wedding. She would never be the same again. But for David…

There was no question in her mind that he had enjoyed their lovemaking. But she must not let herself forget that for him the night had not been the same blinding epiphany it had been for her. She must, she told herself, put a guard on what she said and how she acted.

She felt foolish enough as it was—for not recognizing what was happening to her, for not knowing the difference between infatuation and love. But if David were to realize what she had done…

He wouldn't believe her, of course. Why should he? How could he, when she'd been so wrong when she'd thought she was in love with Travis? She couldn't possibly explain what was so different this time, and she couldn't stand for David to look at her with skepticism. She could see the doubting arch of his eyebrows even now, and the picture sent shivers through her.

But perhaps even worse, he wouldn't want to believe her. Falling in love hadn't been part of the contract. That kind of emotional upheaval led to things like jealousy and watchfulness and questions—all things that David hadn't planned on.

So she must—she absolutely must—keep a rein on her

feelings, and she must keep her newfound knowledge to herself. She would savor it in her heart, and she would not be jealous. She would not watch his every move. She would not ask questions.

The resolution, necessary though it was, took a good deal of the joy out of her heart. Quietly Eve slipped out of bed and padded the length of the apartment to the kitchen.

The skillet full of salmon, lemon, and dill still stood on the burner where they'd left it, looking sadly the worse for wear. Eve made a face as she flushed it down the garbage disposal. Then she started the coffeepot and began to dig in the refrigerator. David would no doubt be amused that she was not only planning to eat breakfast this morning but she was actually cooking it. The very thought of his laugh sent a little ripple of happiness through her.

While she waited for the omelette pan to heat, she started to sort out the contents of the skillet she'd carried in from the living room the night before. The dehydrated potatoes and the can of chicken noodle soup went on the shelf, the can opener and corkscrew into a drawer, the orphaned jar lid and the half-melted plastic box into the garbage can. She tossed the rubber spatula, too, but reconsidered and dug it out again. If David's single knife was so valuable to him, then he might prize his worn-out spatula, as well.

The papers were not as easy to deal with, because if there was anything important in that mess, she certainly wasn't going to recognize it. Eve settled for gathering everything up and stuffing it back between the covers of the week-by-week calendar for David to deal with.

Behind her, the omelette pan sizzled ominously, and as she swung around to check it the calendar slid out of her hand. Papers swirled in every direction, and Eve swore, set the pan off the burner, and began to pick up the pieces.

She was almost finished when she saw it. She didn't know what first caught her eye and made this scrap seem to stand out from the rest. The fact that it had been cut from a newspaper instead of torn, perhaps. But as soon as she picked it up and saw the picture of a smiling couple, there was no question of laying it aside.

For the man in the photograph was David. And the story, from the society page of a newspaper, announced his engagement.

But not to Eve. According to the society page, he intended to marry a woman named Laura Benedict, and the wedding date, the story gushed, had been set for November.

In other words, Eve thought, right about…now.

CHAPTER TEN

EVE stood frozen, looking at the clipping in her hand. No wonder he'd known what veils were made of, she thought wearily. No wonder he'd been relieved that she didn't want an elaborate wedding—the kind people had when they were in love. It would have been too much of a reminder of the wedding he'd planned to have.

But finally her brain began to function again. "The wedding date has been set for November," the story said. *It could have been last November,* she told herself. Or any November in the last several years. There was no date on the bit of newspaper, and from the looks of things, he hadn't thrown away a scrap of paper in that whole length of time…

It doesn't have anything to do with me, she told herself. She wasn't such a fool as to believe she was the first woman in his life. She knew perfectly well she wasn't—she had known it at least since the first time he'd kissed her. She even remembered wondering where he'd learned how to do it so well…

As early as that first kiss, she realized with a sick knot in the pit of her stomach, she'd been feeling the pinch of jealousy. She just hadn't recognized it.

And they'd joked about his supposed dozen live-in lovers. She hadn't believed for a moment there had actually been twelve of them—David had clearly been teasing about that. But had he talked lightly of a dozen in order to deflect her from thinking about the possibility of one in particular?

Eve remembered wondering about that, too—whether there had been a woman in his life who was truly significant. But the anonymous woman she had imagined had been easy to dismiss from her mind. Laura Benedict—blond, pretty, smiling Laura Benedict—wasn't.

I haven't asked you about the women in your life, she had shot at him once. Rather than answering, he had turned the conversation back to Travis.

Well, now she had her answer.

Get over it, she told herself. *For whatever reason, he didn't marry Laura Benedict. He married you.*

Which meant that Laura Benedict didn't matter now, any more than Travis Tate did. They were both in the past. If there had been anything important about it, anything which gave David guilty twinges, he wouldn't have left that newspaper clipping lying around. Or, last night when she'd carried the skillet full of odds and ends into the kitchen, he'd have made some excuse to take the calendar before she could look at it. It would have been easy enough.

If he even knew the story was there. If he hadn't forgotten it, along with the grocery lists and the phone numbers with no names attached.

And, she remembered, there hadn't been much of a chance for him even to notice the calendar last night. It had been in the bottom of the skillet, so he might not even have seen it. Besides, she'd hardly gotten into the kitchen before her accident with the knife. And just as soon as he'd finished bandaging her hand, she'd made the move to seduce him…

"You're going to drive yourself nuts like this," she said aloud. But she had to know. Her hands were trembling as she picked up the calendar again and began to turn the pages, looking carefully at every day in November.

She wanted so much for it not to be there that at first she didn't see it. She actually flipped past the page and had to turn back. But there it was, in fine, firm writing that definitely wasn't David's. It was, instead, a feminine hand which had made the note that his wedding was scheduled for the upcoming weekend.

Well, obviously that wasn't going to happen. But only because Eve had come along instead. Or, rather, because Henry had.

Her own words came back to haunt her. *To be Henry Birmingham's hand-picked successor is a solid-gold opportunity. Any designer with sense would gladly give an arm for this. It would be very foolish of you to walk away.*

Whatever else David might be, he wasn't foolish. And so he had walked away from Laura Benedict instead.

Or had he?

Was she waiting for him, as Eve herself had so faithfully waited for Travis? Had David spun her the same kinds of stories, about a chilly wife and a loveless marriage…?

Except that David's stories, unlike Travis's, would be true.

No, she thought violently. *He wouldn't have asked me to make love with him if he was in love with someone else.*

But he hadn't actually asked her to make love, she reminded herself. He had asked her to go to bed with him, and that was an entirely different thing.

David tiptoed across the kitchen, coming up behind Eve as she stood at the stove, and slipped both arms around her waist.

She tensed a little, and he kissed the nape of her neck. "Did I startle you? I'm sorry. I had to touch you to be sure you were real. I thought I was hallucinating for a minute there when I saw you actually cooking breakfast."

She slipped out of his arms to reach for a spatula and lifted the omelette onto a waiting plate. "Your toast should pop up any minute."

David eyed the plate. "You're not eating? You must be famished after last night." He watched, delighted, as she turned slightly pink. "Missing dinner, I mean," he added gently. "I don't suppose the salmon was salvageable."

"No, it looked like chunks of art-gum erasers stewed in a gluey green sauce. And I've already eaten." She put the omelette pan in the sink. "I'm going to have a long shower, so I may not be ready by the time you've finished. Just go on without me this morning."

Why was she behaving so oddly? He kept his voice carefully casual. "And what excuse shall I give Henry for you being late this time?"

"I'm sure you'll think of something that will satisfy him." She left the kitchen.

David gave a soundless whistle. He wasn't at all sure what was going on, but it didn't take an analyst to see that an entirely different woman had been substituted for the one who had lain in his arms last night. And her preoccupation wasn't just a matter of her being anxious to get to work, either, because she obviously wasn't. For her not even to react to the reminder that everyone at Birmingham on State was watching what time they came in...

So what had happened?

Had he disappointed her last night? He hadn't thought so then, and he still didn't. And that wasn't simply a matter of male ego, because now there was no question that under the glacier lay a very active volcano. He'd expected—after her uninhibited behavior last night—that she'd be a bit shy this morning, maybe even embarrassed, and that it would take some teasing to bring her around. But he hadn't anticipated that she'd freeze solid once more.

Was she having second thoughts about sleeping with him, feeling that she was being unfaithful to Travis? Maybe even feeling guilty that she'd enjoyed herself?

Or was it something else altogether? Last night he'd dismissed the fleeting thought that Henry might have had a hand in her changed attitude. But there was something she'd said...

Henry will be happy, she'd murmured.

David had taken it to be a simple statement of fact, because Henry *would* be happy that his design had worked out.

But then she'd added something else, something David had been almost too satiated and relaxed to notice, much less ponder. She had said, very softly, *Now you have everything you want.*

"Is that why you did it, Eve?" he whispered. "Because you thought you had to?"

And where did that leave them this morning?

What was wrong with her? Eve asked herself bitterly as she stood in the shower, waiting till David was gone and it would be safe to come out. Why was she only attracted to men who were already involved with other women? First Travis, and now David...

Though there was really no comparison between the two cases. This time was infinitely worse, because finding out that David had intended to marry someone else hadn't cured her of loving him. Even knowing about Laura Benedict hadn't kept Eve from wanting to turn 'round in his arms this morning and welcome him with a kiss.

She didn't care about his past... But that wasn't true; she cared horribly. Still, Laura Benedict was the past, and Eve was his future. He had made his choice...

No, Eve thought bleakly. She wasn't his future, Birmingham on State was. He hadn't chosen between the two women, but between Laura Benedict and Birmingham on State. The poor woman had never stood a chance.

He would remain faithful to Birmingham on State, Eve had no doubt. Travis had been right about that much, when he'd pointed out that David had too much to lose now to be careless with it. And that meant he would also be faithful to her—at least as he defined faithful—so long as Henry was watching. He would not break his bargain.

And Eve had no reason to break it, either. She was the one who had set the conditions, and David had followed every last one of them to the letter. Even when he'd asked her to sleep with him, he hadn't been underhanded about it. He hadn't threatened or blackmailed or whined.

She was the one who was acting like a spoiled child, wanting to pick up her toys and go home because she didn't like the game anymore—despite the fact that she'd written the rules herself.

Which left her with a choice to make. She could either honor the promise she'd made and at least keep her self-respect, or she could welsh on the deal, break Henry's heart, and cost David his future.

Put like that, of course there was only one thing she could do. She had told him herself that she saw no reason for a marriage to break up, when it was arranged to achieve good and sensible goals. What a prig she must have sounded.

The goals were still good, still sensible, and so she would live with the bargain she had made, bad as it had turned out to be.

But there would be no more madness like last night. If they were going to follow the bargain, they would go back to the original rules.

It was absolutely critical that he talk to Henry as soon as possible—so of course this would be the day that the old man decided to have a leisurely breakfast and a walk in the park before coming to work. David sat at his workbench, trying to concentrate on replacing a broken fastener on a garnet brooch, but his hands were unsteady. When he heard the tap of Henry's cane he dropped his tools and turned in his chair to face the old man. "Henry," he said with relief. "I need a little time with you."

Henry stood beside the workbench, glanced at the bent pin on the back of the brooch, and shook his head. "If you want advice, I'd say it looks as if you're drinking too much coffee these days. That'll make you shaky."

"Coffee's not the reason I'm shaky." David took a deep breath and plunged. He was too anxious to take time for preliminaries, and too impatient to consider a more tactful approach, so he simply blurted it out. "I want to change the terms of our arrangement concerning Birmingham on State."

Henry's eye narrowed. "It's a little late for that, I'd say."

It's much too late, David thought. *But I have to do it anyway.*

"In fact," he said, keeping his voice as steady as he could, "I want to throw out the agreement altogether."

Behind him, something hit the floor with the musical rattle of fine metal. David wheeled around in his chair to see Eve standing only a few yards away from his workbench. At her feet lay a velvet-lined tray which had once held more than a dozen rings. It was empty now, and the rings, freed by their fall, had scattered over the hardwood floor. One was still spinning. She was staring at him as if he'd struck her.

He leaped to his feet. "Eve—"

Henry's hand was clamped on his arm. David knew he could shake off the old man without much effort, but what was the point? Eve was gone; he could hear her hurried footsteps on the stairway and he knew that he couldn't catch her now. The rings lay abandoned where she had dropped them, stones glinting under the strong lights. The rings that she had brought him so he could try out her idea for a bracelet design...

"You're not going anywhere, my boy," Henry said grimly. "Explain yourself. And this had better be good."

Eve knew she should have been relieved that David had made the choice for both of them. Because he had spoken out, she wouldn't have to carry through a charade, and she didn't have to disappoint Henry.

But the shock of what he had said left her feeling only numb. Had being with her—living with her—sleeping with her—been so unbearable for him that he would even sacrifice Birmingham on State in return for his freedom? Had that seemingly playful embrace this morning simply been the last effort he could bring himself to make?

She couldn't face the curious staff at Birmingham on State. She certainly couldn't face Henry right now, because seeing him angry and hurt would be more than she could bear. She'd have to get a grip on herself first.

But she couldn't bear the silence of the apartment, either. She didn't quite know why she found herself at the natural history museum, walking slowly through the gem collection. She hardly saw the stones; she was reliving the last time she'd been there, and the hope which had been such a large part of the day.

She hadn't known it then, of course, but she'd already been well on the way to falling in love with him.

She caught a glimpse of herself reflected in a mirrored display. Was her face really that white with shock, or did she only look that way because the room was so dimly lit to better show off the gems? She held out a hand to see if it really was as shaky as it felt, and her gaze fell on the beveled platinum of her wedding ring.

How quickly it had grown to be a part of her. How naturally it had fit her hand, as if it had always been there.

He really was a genius, she thought dispassionately. With the thickness and depth of that ring, it should have felt heavy. But something about the way he had engineered it meant that it had never weighed her down. And now, she thought, it never would.

Slowly, she slipped the ring off her finger. It was the first time she had actually held it, because it had never been off her hand since he had put it there.

Just yesterday she'd been wishing she had an engage-

ment ring to go with it, if only so she could pretend it
was a symbol of caring. Now she knew that the wedding
ring was every bit as much a travesty as a diamond
would have been.

Had he even made it for her? Or was it the ring he
would have given Laura Benedict? And if so, had Laura
kept the matching engagement ring as a sort of conso-
lation prize?

Perhaps, she thought, the reason that he hadn't seemed
to be working on a ring that first week was because he
hadn't been. Perhaps Jess Morgan had been right after
all that her necklace was the first thing he'd made at
Birmingham on State.

Stop it, she told herself. *Stop torturing yourself. It
doesn't matter now.*

With a feeling of utter finality, Eve put the ring in the
pocket of her suit. And she went home, because she
didn't know where else to go.

The apartment was quiet, but she knew the instant she
walked in that it wasn't empty. He must be down the
hall in the guest room—she wouldn't call it his bedroom
anymore—packing up his things. She hung up her coat
and went into the kitchen.

The teakettle was just starting to boil when David
came in. "Thank heaven you're here," he said. "I was
starting to worry."

Eve didn't bother to ask why he thought it was any
of his business anymore where she went or what she did.
There was no sense in starting a quarrel; at least they
could part without heated words and hurtful accusations
to remember. "I'll stay out of your way while you get
your things together."

He didn't move. "Eve—"

"I guess we should have expected when we built a

house of cards that it would collapse sooner or later.''
She got a tea bag out and rinsed a cup with hot water.

Still he stood there, quietly. Couldn't the man take a
hint? ''Don't let me keep you—''

''From packing,'' he finished. ''Why do you think
that's what I'm doing?''

She almost dropped her cup. ''I should have thought,
after what you said to Henry this morning, that he told
you to get out and never show your face at Birmingham
on State again.''

''He didn't. He reminded me that we—the three of
us—made a contract.''

She looked directly at him for the first time. ''But
that's ridiculous. He can't hold you to it when you want
out. He wouldn't try, because it would be awful. For the
business, for Henry, for you—'' She swallowed hard.
''For me.''

''You didn't seem to think that last night.''

Her hand stilled on the tea bag. ''What do you
mean?''

''You told me, 'Now you have everything you
want.' ''

She shrugged. ''Well, it did look that way, didn't it?
You had the freedom to design whatever you wished,
you had the beginnings of a reputation as Henry's pro-
tégé, you had the promise of a thriving business that
would be yours one day.''

''And last night you gave me the one thing that had
been missing from the package. Yourself.''

''Only you didn't want me, did you?'' She pulled her
wedding ring out of her pocket. ''Here, David.''

He didn't reach for it. ''What makes you think I didn't
want you?'' His voice was low and tense.

She dropped the ring on the counter in front of him.

It landed with a musical clang. "Oh, perhaps I should have phrased it a little differently. Not that it matters." The acid taste of bitterness pushed her onward. Even though she knew it was stupid to ask, she had to know. "There's just one thing, David. Was this wedding ring ever mine at all? Or is it the one you made for her?"

He seemed to have frozen. *"Her?"*

"Laura Benedict." Eve was proud of herself, because her voice was almost steady. "Remember her? The woman you were going to marry next Saturday?"

"Is that what this is all about?"

She was furious. "No, it isn't. You aren't going to shift the blame for this on me. I'm not the one who told Henry I wanted out."

"You didn't tell him because I beat you to it—but you do want out. That was quite clear this morning. Only—it was because of Laura?"

"No," she said defiantly. "But why didn't you tell me about her, if you didn't expect the idea to bother me?"

"Because she doesn't matter."

"Really? If she doesn't matter, why didn't you tell me about her?"

"Dammit, Eve, you're going in circles. If the idea of Laura doesn't bother you, why are you making such a big deal of it? There was no reason to tell you. It was over."

"It was only over because of me. Or—rather—because of Birmingham on State."

"No."

She waited for more, but the silence stretched into forever and still he didn't go on. Finally she said, "That's it? Just *no?* And I'm supposed to take your word for it?"

"You took my word for a lot of other things."

"That was different!" Instantly, she regretted the out-burst, but it was too late.

He was looking at her with a sparkle of speculation in his eyes. "It sure as hell was," he said. "And you're different, too. If you were still the glacier I married, Laura wouldn't have bothered you in the least."

She couldn't quite stop herself from trembling. "I just—" She stopped, not quite sure what she had started to say. *I just don't want you to lie to me? I just hate the thought that there's a woman besides me in your life?* "It doesn't matter anymore. You told Henry you want out."

"So you didn't have to tell him."

"Just stop it with the nobility, would you? I told you, you are *not* going to shift the blame onto me—"

"Dammit, Eve, that's exactly what I'm trying not to do."

"You're saying you did it to protect me from Henry's wrath," she said flatly. "But I don't believe you. I don't think you can honestly stand there and tell me that's the only reason you said it."

He took a deep breath and for a moment Eve thought the world seemed to hang in the balance.

"No," he said slowly. "It's not the only reason. I've been thinking about it for a while."

Agony washed over her. She didn't realize she had once more allowed herself to hope—however feebly—until the possibility was once more snatched away.

"But Laura's got nothing to do with it," David said firmly. "If you must know…well, we'd known each other for a long time, and—"

Eve said crisply, "I don't think I want to hear the details after all."

"Too late. You asked for it, and you're damn well going to listen. Her mother was a society reporter on this little newspaper, and weddings were her big thing. After Laura and I had been dating a while, her mother started hinting about a wedding date. Drove us crazy at first, but after a while we started thinking, why not? We got along fine, and there obviously wasn't any disagreement from her family. So Laura's mother set the date because she said it would take that long to get all the arrangements made, and she put a story in the paper... I suppose that's how you found out about it?"

Eve nodded stiffly. "It fell out of your calendar."

"But the minute we'd told everybody, I knew I couldn't do it. Laura's a great woman, almost like a sister. Which was the problem, of course. It wouldn't have been fair to either of us to settle for what we had. I felt like a jerk, but I told her she deserved better than what I could give her. And she started to cry—"

Eve bit her lip till it ached. *I might actually like this woman,* she thought. *We have so much in common.*

"And she told me that she'd been trying to work up her nerve to break it off because I deserved more than she could give me. So we had a good laugh and went back to the way it used to be, except after that her mother hated me. We were engaged for all of...I don't know, three weeks maybe."

"And luckily for you," Eve mused, "Henry came along and offered you...more."

"Yeah." David's voice was dry. "A whole lot more than I bargained for."

She didn't even want to contemplate that. Besides, he still hadn't answered the original question. "If it wasn't so you could go back to Laura, why did you tell Henry you wanted out of the agreement?"

For a moment she thought he wasn't going to answer.
"It was one thing to make the bargain we did. It was
something else to live by it."

"You can say that again."

He ignored the interruption. "Because I felt like I was
using you. Oh, hell, I *was* using you, Eve. I married you
because of Birmingham on State, and as long as we were
tangled up in the whole package, I knew you'd never
believe that it wasn't because of Birmingham on State
that I wanted to stay married to you."

Eve's heart stopped beating.

"My dad missed the target," he mused. "His advice
was all right, I guess, it just didn't go far enough. He
told me never to date anybody I wouldn't consider marrying. He didn't warn me not to marry anybody I didn't
intend to fall in love with."

Her throat was almost too dry to speak. "So you told
Henry…"

"I was going to tell him I didn't want to be paid off
for marrying you. That Birmingham on State was yours
absolutely, and I'd take my chances at convincing you
that you wanted to keep me around. Not that I intended
to play fair, exactly," he admitted. "Last night, when
you came to me, I thought I'd won the jackpot. And
then this morning…"

"I found the story about Laura," she whispered. "I
could accept it if you didn't love me—even if you could
never love me. I just couldn't bear the idea that there
was a woman you loved instead of me."

He gathered her close and kissed her, and for a long
time she leaned against him, basking in the joy of being
in his arms again.

"You're very well named, you know," he said finally.
"You have no idea how tempting you are, and I didn't

want to admit it—any more than I wanted to admit that I was jealous as hell of Travis Tate at the airport that day, because I knew you'd never have kissed me if you hadn't been trying to impress him.''

She shook her head a little. ''I think I always knew that I wasn't as important to him as he was to me. Or, rather, as important as I thought he was to me. That was probably one of the reasons I agreed to Henry's plan—to build a wall around myself so I couldn't change my mind, because I knew, deep down inside, that he was the worst thing that had ever happened to me.''

''So you weren't getting even with him, last night?''

''You heard about the twins, too?'' He nodded, and Eve smiled a little. ''No. I think he got what he deserved—and it'll be a little harder for him to play the field with four kids to support. But I do owe him something, because that was when I realized what had happened. I didn't feel hurt, because you were taking up all the space I thought I'd saved for Travis.''

''I don't plan to give up an inch of it, either. Now that I have your full attention, I'm not letting go.''

''So what *did* you tell Henry this morning?''

''Everything,'' he said simply. ''I didn't start out to, but eventually he got the whole story. He's a wise old bird, you know. He knew perfectly well what he was doing. Take a man and a woman, isolate them in a small space, and wait for the inevitable.''

''We're incredibly lucky, David.''

''No. Well, yes—but it wasn't only luck. It was Henry. He told me this morning that his list of three candidates was fictitious, that I was the only one he considered—and that he's quite confident we'll make it because he thinks we're perfectly matched. Something about us both being loyal to the core, right past the point of common sense. I'm still not sure whether he meant it as a compliment.''

Eve laughed. ''Probably, but when Henry starts sounding like a saint—''

''He's just about as dangerous as you when you smile. Eve, do you really think I'd have given you a ring that belonged to another woman?''

She didn't answer directly. ''You told Mrs. Morgan that night at the Captain's Table that your first job would be to make a wedding ring—and then you didn't do it.''

''You expected me to let you get a glimpse of it? Besides, it was almost finished when I came out here. It was one of the fastest jobs I've ever done because it seemed to make itself.'' He picked up the ring from where she'd tossed it on the counter and slid it back on her hand.

The platinum band felt cool against her finger. Eve studied it with satisfaction. ''All I knew was that you didn't seem to be working on it. Then when I found out about Laura—''

''You thought I'd just recycled the ring.''

''Even though I was hurt at the idea,'' she said softly, ''I didn't blame you exactly. The way I laid down the law about what I wanted, demanding that you not show off your talent—''

''I really tried to do what you asked, Eve. Plain and simple.''

''And refusing even to consider an engagement ring,'' she added softly.

''Having second thoughts about that, are you?''

She shook her head with determination and held up her hand. ''This is the important one.''

''I don't quite believe you, you know.''

"All right," she admitted. "I do regret it. So will you make me a diamond ring now?"

He kissed her softly and said, "No."

Eve frowned. "Why? If it's because we're already married—"

David reached into his pocket. "It's because you said no diamonds." He held out his hand.

On his palm sparkled a band almost identical to her wedding ring. It was a little wider, and standing high in an almost flamboyant mounting sparkled a dark bluish-green stone, the most beautiful emerald Eve had ever seen.

"However, you did once mention an emerald as big as a traffic light," he murmured. "It seemed a little impractical to have a crane following you around all the time, so I'm afraid you'll have to settle for eleven carats."

She had started to cry. "You made this even before—"

"Before I knew what had hit me, yes. While I was still joking about how this deal might cost me a rib. What I didn't expect was that it would cost me my heart."

"It's so beautiful," she whispered.

"There is one thing you need to know about it before you put it on," he warned. "I'm afraid it's like that ruby necklace our customer was complaining about."

She frowned, trying to remember. "The one that she thinks has a curse?"

"Yeah. Only this emerald really does. It comes with a husband who's so much in love with you that his judgment isn't always very good. And once it's on your finger, it doesn't come off. Will you marry me, Eve? Really marry me?"

"I don't know," she said thoughtfully. "Are you sure you wouldn't rather have an affair? Oh, that's right—you said people who are married to each other can't have affairs."

"I was wrong," he said against her lips. "And I'll prove it to you, if you like."

She smiled and held up her hand so he could slide the ring into place. "I like," she said softly, and then there was nothing else to say.

Modern Romance™
...seduction and
passion guaranteed

Tender Romance™
...love affairs that
last a lifetime

Sensual Romance™
...sassy, sexy and
seductive

Blaze
...sultry days and
steamy nights

Medical Romance™
...medical drama on
the pulse

Historical Romance™
...rich, vivid and
passionate

27 new titles every month.

*With all kinds of Romance for
every kind of mood...*

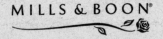

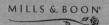

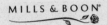

R

2 Books
and a surprise gift!

We would like to take this opportunity to thank you for reading this Mills & Boon® book by offering you the chance to take TWO more specially selected titles from the Tender Romance™ series absolutely FREE! We're also making this offer to introduce you to the benefits of the Reader Service™—

- ★ FREE home delivery
- ★ FREE gifts and competitions
- ★ FREE monthly Newsletter
- ★ Books available before they're in the shops
- ★ Exclusive Reader Service discount

Accepting these FREE books and gift places you under no obligation to buy; you may cancel at any time, even after receiving your free shipment. Simply complete your details below and return the entire page to the address below. *You don't even need a stamp!*

YES! Please send me 2 free Tender Romance books and a surprise gift. I understand that unless you hear from me, I will receive 4 superb new titles every month for just £2.55 each, postage and packing free. I am under no obligation to purchase any books and may cancel my subscription at any time. The free books and gift will be mine to keep in any case.

N2ZEB

Ms/Mrs/Miss/Mr ....Initials.................................
BLOCK CAPITALS PLEASE

Surname...

Address..

....

....Postcode ....

Send this whole page to:
UK: The Reader Service, FREEPOST CN8I, Croydon, CR9 3WZ
EIRE: The Reader Service, PO Box 4546, Kilcock, County Kildare (stamp required)

Offer not valid to current Reader Service subscribers to this series. We reserve the right to refuse an application and applicants must be aged 18 years or over. Only one application per household. Terms and prices subject to change without notice. Offer expires 29th November 2002. As a result of this application, you may receive offers from other carefully selected companies. If you would prefer not to share in this opportunity please write to The Data Manager at the address above.

Mills & Boon® is a registered trademark owned by Harlequin Mills & Boon Limited.
Tender Romance ™ is being used as a trademark.